Gwyneth Rees is half Welsh and half English and grew up in Scotland. She went to Glasgow University and qualified as a doctor in 1990. She is a child and adolescent psychiatrist but has now stopped practising so that she can write full-time. She is the author of the bestselling Fairies series (*Fairy Dust*, *Fairy Treasure*, *Fairy Dreams*, *Fairy Gold*, *Fairy Rescue*), *Cosmo and the Magic Sneeze*, *Cosmo and the Great Witch Escape* and *Mermaid Magic*, as well as several books for older readers. She lives in London with her two cats.

Visit www.gwynethrees.com

# fairy rescue

The fairies are in danger!

## Gwyneth Rees

Illustrated by Emily Bannister

MACMILLAN CHILDREN'S BOOKS

First published 2007 by Macmillan Children's Books
a division of Macmillan Publishers Limited
20 New Wharf Road, London N1 9RR
Basingstoke and Oxford
www.panmacmillan.com

Associated companies throughout the world

ISBN: 978-0-330-43971-8

1 3 5 7 9 8 6 4 2

A CIP catalogue record for this book is available from
the British Library.

Typeset by Nigel Hazle
Printed and bound in Great Britain by Mackays of Chatham plc, Kent

*For Yi Lan Taylor and Megan Shaw*
*and their favourite dog, Milo,*
*with lots of love*

*1*

Maddie felt as if she was in a special magical land as she weaved her way in and out of the trees, just out of sight of the main path that ran through the woods behind her grandparents' house. She could hear Grandpa talking to his dog, Milo, as he walked along the path, but otherwise the woods were silent.

It was a sunny day and rays of light were penetrating the leafy roof above her. Maddie was pretending to be a flower fairy who lived deep in the forest and she

was searching for some suitable flowers to wear as a garland in her hair. Maddie had long light brown hair which was curly at the ends, and which she usually tied back in a ponytail to keep off her face. Today it kept getting caught on twigs as she walked under the trees.

After she had made a yellow crown out of some long-stemmed buttercups, she joined her grandfather on the path. Grandpa had just thrown a stick for Milo to fetch and Milo, who was a very excitable Jack Russell terrier, was barking loudly as he ran off into the woods after it.

'I really like going for walks with you, Grandpa,' Maddie told him, slipping her hand into his. 'When Mum's with me she won't let me do *anything*.' Maddie's mum had come with them yesterday on their afternoon walk, and she had fussed

over Maddie the whole time. She had been too worried to let Maddie run off into the woods after Milo and she had nearly had a fit when Maddie started to climb a tree.

'Your mum's just worried in case you get ill again,' Grandpa said. 'I'm sure she doesn't mean to spoil your fun.'

'Well, she *does* spoil it,' Maddie said crossly. 'She spoils everything. She treats me like a baby and it's not fair!'

'She's just feeling very protective of you because of what happened,' Grandpa said. 'She'll get over it. You just need to give her some time. Now ... I wonder what's happened to Milo.'

Milo hadn't returned with the stick, and he wasn't barking any more either. They waited for several minutes but he still didn't return, even when Grandpa called him.

'Do you think he's all right?' Maddie asked.

Grandpa didn't look too concerned. 'He might have found a rabbit hole or something. Why don't you go and have a look for him? Don't go too far though. Give me a shout when you find him.'

So Maddie set off into the woods and soon spotted Milo crouching on the ground next to a large tree stump. His bottom was sticking up in the air and his black-and-white stumpy tail was wagging furiously. Maddie was about to shout out to tell Grandpa she had found him when

4

she saw that Milo had spotted something in the grass. Whatever it was, Milo seemed fascinated by it. At first Maddie couldn't see what he was looking at, but then the object moved suddenly and Maddie saw a flash of yellow whizz across the ground and dart away through the trees. Before Maddie had time to shout out, she heard a noise behind her and her grandfather appeared.

Milo started to roll about on the ground, yapping with excitement again, as Maddie told Grandpa what she had seen.

'It must have been a butterfly,' Grandpa said.

'I don't think it was,' Maddie said, frowning.

'Or maybe it was a fairy,' Grandpa teased. 'Some folks say that they live in these woods.'

'*Really?*' Maddie had always believed

in fairies, but she had never actually seen one.

'They say that if you believe in fairies and you come for a walk here often enough, you're bound to see one sooner or later,' Grandpa said, smiling at her.

Maddie looked at Milo, who was now sitting up, wagging his tail. 'I wonder if *Milo* believes in fairies,' she said.

Grandpa laughed.

'I mean it, Grandpa,' she said solemnly. 'Aunt Rachel told me that you can only see fairies if you believe in them, so if Milo believes in fairies it means he'll be able to see them, which means it really *could* have been a fairy he was looking at just now.' Aunt Rachel was her mother's sister, and she was the only one in the family, apart from Maddie, who believed that fairies were real.

Grandpa was still smiling, but Maddie was looking very thoughtful now.

'Milo, *do* you believe in fairies?' she asked, crouching down in front of the little dog and looking straight into his eyes.

Milo cocked his head and pricked up his ears and his tail started wagging furiously. And as Maddie stared at his eyes, she thought she saw, reflected in them, a tiny fairy in a yellow petal dress.

She instantly looked around her, but there was no sign of a fairy or anything else. Maybe she was imagining things.

'We'd better be going now,' Grandpa said, starting to lead the way back to the path.

As they got there, they heard heavy footsteps approaching, and suddenly an elderly man (who looked about the same age as Grandpa) appeared. He was dressed

in an old-fashioned brown tweed suit and he was carrying a large canvas bag over one shoulder.

'Hello, Horace,' Grandpa said, not sounding at all surprised to see him. 'Maddie, this is Mr Hatter. He lives along the road from us. His garden backs on to the woods too.'

Horace Hatter frowned as if he didn't really have time to stop and chat.

Grandpa didn't take the hint though. 'Horace and I were at school together,' he told Maddie. 'We were both in the stamp-collecting club – not that my collection was anything like as impressive as Horace's.' He chuckled. 'Horace was always mad about collecting things. If it wasn't stamps or coins, it was birds' eggs or butterflies. Isn't that right, Horace?'

'Once a collector, always a collector,' Horace grunted.

'Did you let the butterflies go after you caught them?' Maddie asked, not liking the thought of butterflies being captured.

Horace looked at her as if he thought she was very stupid. 'Of course I didn't let them go. I have twenty glass cases full of them – all correctly labelled. I can't abide collectors who don't label things,' he added, glancing at Grandpa, who he still remembered had kept *his* stamp collection in an old envelope when they were boys. 'If you don't mind, I'd better be getting on,' he said curtly, brushing past them to continue along the path.

'He's not very friendly, is he?' Maddie whispered as soon as he was out of sight.

Grandpa laughed. 'He was always a bit eccentric, was old Horace. Don't worry. He

hasn't collected butterflies in a long time. Now . . . You and I had better start heading back. We've already stayed out longer than I meant to. We don't want your mum to start worrying about you, do we?'

'Mum's *always* worrying about me, so what difference does it make?' Maddie said impatiently.

'Come on, Maddie. You're very precious to her – you know that.'

Maddie pulled a face and was about to reply when she spotted a streak of yellow whizzing past the dark green leaves of a nearby tree. She was lifting her hand to point it out to Grandpa when a ray of sunlight broke through the trees and shone straight into her eyes. When she escaped from its glare she couldn't see anything up in the treetops except greenery.

Slowly she followed her grandfather

back along the narrow path towards home, still thinking about fairies. And though she didn't know it, a flower fairy in a yellow petal dress was now using the ray of sunlight as a slide, shrieking with delight as she slid down it and landed with a bump on the springy mossy floor.

Maddie's mother was waiting anxiously for them when they arrived back.

Maddie had been hoping Mum would relax when they got to Grandma and Grandpa's cosy house in the country, and she knew her dad had been hoping

the same thing. (It was Dad who had suggested they came to stay here for the summer – he was coming to join them in a few weeks' time when he was on holiday from work.) But so far – and they had been here for nearly a week – Mum was being as overprotective as ever.

Maddie had had to plead with her to be allowed to go out with Grandpa and Milo that afternoon. 'What if you get an asthma attack again?' Mum had said, looking worried. 'How will Grandpa get help if the two of you are alone in the middle of the woods?'

'I'll have my inhaler with me,' Maddie had protested. 'I'll be fine.'

And she'd been right, hadn't she? She *was* fine. But just because they had arrived home a bit later than expected, Mum had got herself all worked up as usual.

Mum had always worried a lot about Maddie, but the reason she had been especially anxious recently was that that spring Maddie, who had suffered from asthma since she was tiny, had caught a nasty chest infection. It had triggered a flare-up of her asthma and one evening, when Maddie and her mum were alone in the house, Maddie had become so wheezy that her inhaler hadn't helped. Her mum had called an ambulance and Maddie had been taken to hospital immediately, but by the time they got there she'd been so ill that she'd had to be admitted to intensive care.

She was completely better now – apart from having to use her inhaler in the same way she had always used it – but her mum still hadn't recovered from the shock. Now if Maddie got even the slightest bit wheezy, Mum immediately panicked, and

13

she always got very twitchy if Maddie was out of her sight for too long.

'We aren't that late,' Grandpa told Mum. 'And I'm sure the fresh air and exercise will have done Maddie good. Anyway, didn't the doctors say that you should carry on as normal now that she's well again?'

'It's easy for *you* to stay calm,' Mum retorted sharply. '*You* weren't there when . . .' She broke off abruptly and her eyes filled up with tears, as they always did when she remembered the night when Maddie had been rushed to hospital in an ambulance.

But for once Maddie's eyes were filling up with tears too. 'I'm *better* now, Mum,' she snapped, 'and I hate you treating me like I'm different to everybody else!' And she stomped out of the room.

14

After that Maddie's mum didn't say any more about Grandpa and Maddie being late home, and that evening as they sat round the table to eat together Grandpa told the others about the yellow fluttery thing that Maddie had seen in the woods. 'I told her it was probably a fairy,' he said, winking at Grandma.

Mum smiled at that. 'Do you remember when Rachel took me off into the woods in the middle of the night because she said the fairies had invited us to a party?'

'I didn't know about it until the morning,' Grandma said, 'or I'd never have let you go. You were only five. Rachel was nine – old enough to know better. I mean, what if the two of you had got lost? By the way, a parcel arrived from your Aunt Rachel while you were out, Maddie. It's for your birthday, I expect.' Aunt Rachel lived a long way away so they didn't see her very often, but she always remembered Maddie's birthday.

Maddie was going to be nine years old in a few days' time, and usually whenever anyone mentioned that, she got very excited. But right now she was totally transfixed by Mum's story about the fairy party.

'Did you *see* any fairies, Mum?' she asked excitedly.

'I fell asleep when we got to the fairy grove. Rachel said she tried to wake me up when the fairies appeared but she couldn't, so she left me sleeping and went to join the party. She said she met the fairy queen, but I didn't really believe her.'

'Our Rachel always had a great imagination,' Grandma said.

Mum nodded. 'She certainly did. I remember she told me the fairies were celebrating the anniversary of the day they first came to live in these woods, hundreds of years ago!'

'When *was* the anniversary?' Maddie asked excitedly.

'I guess it was round about now,' Mum said. 'It was definitely right in the middle of the summer, because I remember it was a lovely warm night.'

'Maybe the fairies are having a party *this* summer too,' Maddie exclaimed. 'Maybe they have one *every* year, the way people have birthday parties!'

'Here's another one with a big imagination,' Grandma said, and the three grown-ups all smiled at her indulgently.

The next morning Maddie and Grandpa took Milo for another walk through the woods.

'Where's the fairy grove Mum was talking about last night?' Maddie asked as they watched Milo race off along the path after a stick.

'There's a long stream that runs through these woods and at some point it's supposed to run through a magic clearing where the fairies have their gatherings. Folks call that place the fairy grove. But it's said that only people who believe in fairies can find it.'

'*I* believe in fairies,' Maddie pointed out.

'I'm not sure we've got time to look for it now. We promised we'd make sure we were back for lunch, didn't we?'

'*Please*, Grandpa. Just a *little* look.' Maddie tugged at his hand and put on her most pleading expression, which rarely worked with Mum but nearly always did with her grandfather.

'Well, how about I take you to see the stream now? Will that do?'

Maddie nodded excitedly, so Grandpa led her away from the path and into the thicker part of the woods. Milo followed at their heels, his ears pricked up attentively. Eventually, when they had been walking for a good five minutes, they heard a gentle gurgling sound.

'Maybe you'd better wait here, Grandpa,' Maddie said as they reached the stream, which looked cool and fresh and had very

sparkly water. 'You don't believe in fairies, so we might not find the fairy grove if you come with me.' She started to take off her sandals so that she could walk along in the stream itself, which was only ankle deep. 'Milo had better stay here too in case he scares the fairies away.'

Grandpa chuckled as he got out Milo's lead and clipped it on to his collar. 'You can take five minutes to look for it,' he said, 'but then we really must head back. I'll wait here for you. You've still got your inhaler in your pocket, haven't you?'

Maddie nodded, taking it out to show him. Then she set off along the stream, taking care as she picked her way over the mossy pebbles. Soon the stream turned a corner so that she was out of sight of her grandfather and it was then that she heard the tiny voices arguing.

'It's not fair! Why can't I go?' a little high-pitched voice was protesting crossly.

'Poppy, you know you aren't allowed. What if you fall off?'

'I won't fall off!'

'You might! Birds fly very fast, you know! Anyway, it's our job to look after you and that means you can't go anywhere without us.'

As Maddie stood absolutely still she saw three fairies standing on the bank next to the stream. Each one was small enough to sit in the palm of Maddie's hand and they were all wearing delicate petal dresses. One fairy was facing her. She wore a red poppy-petal dress that was short and flouncy and she had long smooth black hair, which she was flicking off her face in an angry manner.

The other two fairies, who were standing with their backs to Maddie, were both blonde. One wore a white dress made from long thin daisy petals, and the other wore a yellow dress made of primrose petals. Their wings were almost transparent, like insects' wings, except that they were much bigger

and they sparkled. Maddie wondered if the yellow fairy was the same one she had seen flying through the woods the previous day.

The fairy called Poppy was the first one to notice her standing there. 'Uh-oh!' she sang out in a warning voice, pointing at Maddie.

The other two fairies turned to face her, looking alarmed.

'Please don't be frightened,' Maddie said quickly. 'I won't hurt you. I *love* fairies!'

'Oh – have you met some before then?' Poppy asked swiftly. She seemed the boldest of the three, Maddie thought.

'Well . . . no . . . but I've always loved the *idea* of fairies.'

Poppy nodded as if she understood. 'I used to love the *idea* of children,' she said. 'Before I met any, that is.'

23

'Oh . . . don't you like children any more?' Maddie asked her in dismay.

Poppy looked very solemn now, lowering her voice slightly, as if she was about to tell Maddie a secret. 'You've heard of bad children pulling the wings off flies, haven't you?'

Maddie nodded, frowning. She had never actually seen anyone do that, but once a boy in the year above her at school had chopped an earthworm in half in the playground. That had made her feel quite sick.

And that's when Poppy spun round and Maddie saw that she had only one wing.

Maddie was horrified. 'Did a *child* do that to you?'

Before she could answer, the other two fairies broke in.

'Stop teasing her, Poppy!'

'No one pulled off her wing – she was born that way!'

'Why do you always have to be so silly about it, Poppy?'

The other two fairies were glaring at Poppy, who didn't seem the least bit ashamed of lying. In fact, she looked highly amused by the expression on Maddie's face.

Maddie felt cross for a moment, but then, all of a sudden, she thought she understood Poppy. After all, she knew what it was like to have everyone feeling sorry for you and treating you like you were different the whole time. 'I expect you joke about it so that people don't feel sorry for you, don't you?' she said.

Poppy stared at Maddie in surprise.

'I'm Maddie, by the way.'

'We're Primrose, Daisy and Poppy,' the yellow fairy said. 'We're meant to be inviting all the woodland animals to our party tonight, and a very kind thrush just offered to give Poppy a ride through the woods on her back. But Poppy's not allowed to ride on birds' backs in case she falls off. Poppy can't fly, you see.'

Maddie looked at Poppy's single wing and noticed that it wasn't sparkling like the other fairies' wings. 'Can't you fly at all?' she asked her.

Poppy shook her head. 'The others have to carry me everywhere. But I don't see why

I can't go for a ride on a thrush if I want to.'

'We've already told you why!' Primrose said impatiently. 'Imagine how we'd feel if anything happened to you. And imagine what Queen Flora would say!'

'Who's Queen Flora?' Maddie asked.

'She's our fairy queen,' Poppy explained. 'She fusses over me something rotten on account of my wing. She's put Daisy and Primrose in charge of looking after me and I'm not allowed to go anywhere without them.'

'Your fairy queen sounds a bit like my mother,' Maddie said sympathetically. 'She fusses over *me* because of my asthma and because when I was born—' She broke off abruptly as she heard Grandpa calling her name. 'I'd better go now, but . . .' She hesitated, feeling very shy all of a sudden.

'... I was wondering ... You know how you said you were having a fairy party to celebrate when the fairies first came to live in these woods?'

'How do *you* know that's what we're celebrating?' Primrose sounded suspicious. 'We never told you that!'

Maddie flushed. 'My mum told me about it. You see, *she* came to a fairy party in these woods when *she* was a little girl. Her big sister brought her.'

Daisy's face lit up suddenly. 'I think I remember those two little girls. The older one came and danced with us while her little sister slept the whole night. The little one didn't believe in fairies – that's why she didn't wake up in the fairy grove.'

Maddie stared at Daisy. 'You actually *remember* them?'

'Of course. Why shouldn't I?'

'Because ... well ... Mum and Aunt Rachel are grown-up now and you're ... you're ...'

Daisy laughed. 'I'm ancient,' she said. 'I may not look it, but I'm over a hundred years old. Fairies can live for a very long time, you know.'

'Wow!' Maddie was about to ask Poppy and Primrose how old *they* were when they heard Grandpa's voice again. This time he sounded much closer. 'I'd better go,' Maddie said. 'But if I come back to the woods tonight, will I be allowed to come to your party like my auntie and my mum did?'

'I don't see why not,' said Poppy. 'Come to the woods at midnight and we'll be having our party here in the fairy grove. We'll leave you a trail of fairy dust to follow so you can find us.'

'Thank you,' Maddie said, beaming at them. She was about to go when she remembered her manners. 'Would you like me to bring anything to the party?' she asked politely.

The three fairies looked at each other, clearly delighted that she had offered.

'CHOCOLATE!' they sang out in unison.

'Do fairies like chocolate then?' Maddie asked in surprise.

'Of course!' Primrose told her. 'All fairies *love* chocolate.'

'And we can't get it in fairyland,' Poppy added, 'which is why children can come in quite useful sometimes.'

'Not that we only like children because they bring us chocolate,' Daisy put in quickly.

Maddie laughed. 'Is *fairyland* where you

live then?' she said. 'I thought you lived in the woods.'

'Fairyland *is* in the woods, silly! It's—' Poppy broke off as Grandpa appeared round the corner with Milo. 'Oops! Come on you two, we'd better go!'

Maddie watched as the three fairies flew off into the tree tops – Daisy and Primrose on either side of Poppy with their arms linked through hers.

Grandpa wasn't looking very pleased. 'Maddie, didn't you hear me calling you? We'll be late for lunch if we don't go home now.'

Maddie half-expected Grandpa to notice the fairies flying away, but he didn't seem to be able to see them. Milo, however, was looking up into the treetops, barking and wagging his tail excitedly. Maddie almost told Grandpa everything, but something

made her decide to keep it to herself, at least for now.

On their way home they met Horace Hatter walking towards them along the path. He was carrying a butterfly net today, as well as his canvas backpack.

'I thought you said he didn't collect butterflies any more,' Maddie whispered to her grandfather.

'Well, that's what he told me last time I asked him about it – said it was more his father's thing, in any case – the butterfly-collecting.' Grandpa grinned at Horace as they drew level. 'Morning, Horace! Or is it afternoon by now?'

Horace grunted something back at him, not sounding particularly friendly.

'I didn't know you still collected butterflies,' Grandpa said. 'Isn't it illegal now?'

Horace scowled at him. 'I'm not looking for butterflies,' he said curtly. And he stepped around them and marched on along the path.

**3**

That night Maddie went to bed early and silently willed her mother to do the same. Her grandparents weren't a problem, because they were always in bed with the light off by half past ten, but Mum sometimes stayed up much later. And if she did that tonight, Maddie was going to have trouble sneaking out of the house.

Before she got into bed Maddie got changed – but not into her pyjamas. Instead she put on her best dress, the one she had brought with her to wear on her birthday. It

was pink with yellow flowers on it and she had pink sparkly shoes to wear too. She was planning on wearing her sandals to walk to the party and changing into her sparkly shoes when she got there, so she put the shoes into her favourite glittery bag. Inside the bag she also put the chocolate she had bought for the party, which consisted of several packets of chocolate buttons and some chocolate-coated nuts. She reckoned the fairies would like the chocolate buttons, and that the nuts would be perfect if any squirrels had been invited – which she hoped they had because she loved squirrels.

She lay down fully dressed under the covers and somehow managed to keep herself awake long enough to hear her mum go into her bedroom at just after half past eleven. Normally Maddie would be fast asleep by that time and she reckoned it must be the excitement that was keeping her so alert. In fact she was so excited that she forgot to take her inhaler with her as she picked up her bag and left her room to creep downstairs.

She remembered the inhaler just as she was about to close the back door behind her, but as she crept back into the house to fetch it she heard movement on the landing. She stopped where she was. It was now or never if she wanted to leave without being caught. Silently she slipped out through the back door and tiptoed across the garden, certain that she wouldn't need her inhaler in any case. After all, she usually only got breathless if she was upset or if she'd been running about too much – and she didn't see that she'd be doing either at a fairy party.

The moon was out so it was easy to see

her way. There was a gate at the bottom of the garden that led into the woods behind the house, which was the way she and Grandpa always went when they took Milo for a walk. She was glad Milo wasn't with her tonight because, much as she loved him, she was sure he would make too much noise. (Luckily he always slept in her grandparents' bedroom so he hadn't been in the kitchen to bark at her when she'd left the house.)

The fairies had told her she would find fairy dust – whatever *that* was – to guide her to the party, so she started to look for it as she entered the woods. She was beginning to worry that she wouldn't be able to see anything soon because the trees were blocking out the moonlight, but then she saw something on the path just ahead of her. It was an arrow made of sparkly dust!

She followed the direction of the arrow – which meant stepping off the path – and immediately ahead of her she saw another arrow. It was on a tree trunk this time and it was giving off such a powerful glow that the area around it was completely lit up.

There turned out to be a sparkly arrow on every second or third tree she came to, so

it was impossible to mistake the direction she was meant to take.

She had been following the sparkly arrows for about five minutes when they suddenly stopped. She could still see because the moonlight seemed to be penetrating the trees here, and she could hear the sound of the stream nearby. She guessed that she was quite near the fairy grove, but she couldn't hear any noise that sounded like a party.

Suddenly the moon disappeared behind a cloud and she was in total darkness.

That was when she began to feel scared. There was clearly no party anywhere nearby, and even as her eyes began to grow accustomed to the dark she couldn't see anything except the trees looming up around her. Had the fairies been playing some sort of trick on her? She felt her chest getting tighter and her breath seemed to be

coming less easily. Automatically she felt in her pocket for her inhaler, but of course she didn't have it with her.

Just then a light appeared in the trees above her and a fairy she had never seen before appeared. Maddie gasped. The fairy was surrounded by a rainbow-coloured glow, and as she came closer Maddie saw that she was dressed in a magnificent multicoloured petal dress. She had beautiful sparkling wings and violet-petal slippers, and on her head was a crown made from forest flowers. Her delicate shawl was woven from the finest spider's-web thread, which had been coated in morning dew to make it glisten.

'I am Queen Flora – queen of the flower fairies,' she said in a sweet, clear voice. 'Are you Maddie?'

'Y-y-yes,' Maddie stammered, still struggling to breathe properly.

The fairy queen saw at once that Maddie was distressed. 'Don't worry, you're quite safe now,' she said. And to Maddie's surprise the fairy queen began to sing. It was some sort of fairy lullaby and it was so gentle and soothing that Maddie soon found that her breathing was coming a little easier.

'I forgot my . . . inhaler,' she whispered. 'It . . . helps me breathe.'

Queen Flora looked worried. 'Where is this object? I will fetch it for you.'

'It's on the table ... beside my bed. It's a sort of ... plastic ... puffer thing. But I don't ... want you ... to go.' Her chest immediately felt much tighter at the thought of being left alone in the darkness.

Queen Flora began to sing again until Maddie had become calmer. 'Now sit here against this tree and close your eyes,' the fairy queen ordered, 'and keep that tune inside your head until I return. Which house do you live in?'

Maddie told her.

'Do as I say and I shall be back before you know it.'

So Maddie did as she was told. She kept her eyes closed and played the lullaby over and over inside her head. It was almost as if the fairy lullaby was able to speed up time because, much sooner than she had expected, the fairy queen returned and was dropping her inhaler into her lap.

Gratefully Maddie picked it up and put it to her mouth and as Queen Flora looked on she took in the puffs of medicine.

'You know, you're a very silly girl to come into the woods in the middle of the night without this object,' the fairy queen said, when she was sure that Maddie was feeling better.

'I forgot it because I was so excited about the fairy party,' Maddie explained. 'Poppy, Primrose and Daisy invited me, but I couldn't find the party and then it went dark and I got scared.'

'I'm afraid we have had to cancel the fairy party,' Queen Flora said.

'Oh no! *Why?*'

Queen Flora looked solemn. 'Poppy,

Primrose and Daisy have disappeared. They didn't return from the woods this evening after they came here to set up those arrows for you. We have looked everywhere for them, and while we were looking we found something very frightening.'

'What?'

'Come. I will show you.' She led Maddie towards the sound of the stream, then stopped suddenly at one particular tree. 'Look,' she said, flying up to hover in front of it.

The moon was fully out from behind the clouds and the trees had thinned out a little now that they were almost at the fairy grove. In the moonlight Maddie saw that one of the tree's lower branches had been snapped off.

'Under this tree we found a poppy petal,' Queen Flora said.

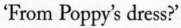

'From Poppy's dress?'

'There are no other poppies in these woods. But look what we found on the part of the branch that is left.'

The branch wasn't very high up. Maddie couldn't see anything at first. Then she reached up and touched the surface. To her surprise she found that what remained of the branch was incredibly sticky. She pulled her hand away quickly and rubbed it on some nearby leaves. She gasped. 'What *is* it?'

'Bird-lime,' Queen Flora told her. 'It's a very old method used to trap wild birds. The trapper spreads the bird-lime – which is very sticky – on a bird's favourite perch and when the bird next sits there it gets the bird-lime on its feet or on its wings and it can't move until it's released by the trapper, who cleans the bird and puts it in a cage.'

'But why would anyone want to do that?'

'A long time ago a lot of people kept songbirds in cages in their homes, so there was quite a market in them. Now that doesn't happen so much. But this trapper must be targeting fairies instead. This branch was a favourite spot for those three.'

'But who would want to catch a *fairy*?' Maddie exclaimed.

'I have no idea, but I have called a meeting of the Fairy High Council to plan what we should do.'

'That sounds important,' Maddie said in an awed voice.

'The Fairy High Council is a special group made up of all the fairy queens from across the country,' Queen Flora explained. 'We only meet if there is a very serious fairy incident to discuss.'

'Will the meeting happen *here*?' Maddie asked, thinking it might be a very interesting sort of meeting to attend.

'It will take place on the Isle of Skye in Scotland, where the oldest flower-fairy community lives. The fairy queen there is called Queen Mae and she is a very good friend of mine. I shall go there at sunrise tomorrow, and while I am away I shall seal off the entrance to fairyland in these woods, to protect the rest of my fairies.'

'Where *is* the entrance to fairyland exactly?' Maddie asked curiously.

'I think I have told you enough, my dear. Now it is time for me to go, but first I will escort you home.'

Together Maddie and Queen Flora retraced Maddie's earlier journey – with the fairy queen leading the way since the arrows had all gone. When they reached

the bottom of Maddie's garden the fairy queen said goodbye. 'Keep a lookout for my missing fairies, won't you?'

Maddie promised that she would and immediately made up her mind to enlist Milo's help the following day. After all, the police used dogs to help find missing people, so why shouldn't she use Milo to help find the missing fairies?

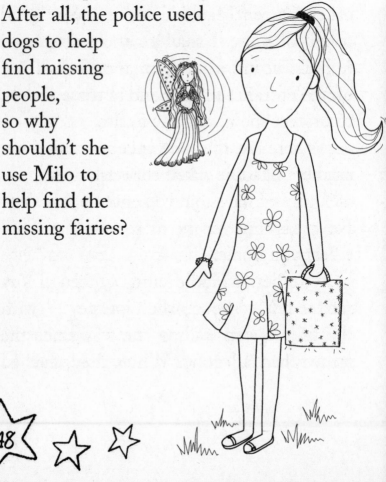

4

As Maddie crossed the garden she noticed a chink of light in the kitchen window and when she got to the house she peered inside through the gap in the curtains. Her mother and grandmother were sitting at the kitchen table and Grandma had her arm around Mum.

Maddie opened the back door immediately and said, 'It's all right, Mum. I'm quite safe. I just went for a walk.'

'Maddie! Thank goodness!' her mum cried out, rushing over to clutch Maddie in

her arms. Her eyes were red and it was clear she had been crying.

'Your grandfather's out looking for you,' Grandma told Maddie sharply. 'You've scared your mother half to death!'

'I'm sorry, Mum!' Maddie burst out. 'But you'll never guess what's happened ...' And she began to tell them all about the missing fairies.

Unfortunately neither Mum nor Grandma – nor Grandpa when he got home – believed her story, and her mother was horrified when she heard Maddie had gone into the woods all alone.

'What if something had happened to you?' Mum gasped.

'But it didn't,' Maddie pointed out.

'Yes, but it _could_ have ...' Her voice cracked and she covered her face with her hands as if she couldn't even bear to think

about all the bad things that might have happened.

Maddie didn't know what to say. For some reason she found herself thinking about the time that spring when she had woken up in hospital, feeling groggy but a lot better, and heard her mum and dad talking quietly as they sat by her bed.

'If we'd lost her too . . .' she'd heard Mum whisper, and Dad had whispered back that Maddie was strong and that they weren't going to lose her.

'I know. I just can't help thinking about Charlotte,' her mother had said.

Maddie had always known that she had originally been one of a set of twins who had been born very prematurely. Because they had been born too soon they were both so small and weak that they had had to be admitted to the babies' intensive-care

unit, where Maddie's twin sister, Charlotte, had died when she was just three weeks old.

Maddie often thought about what it would be like if Charlotte hadn't died, and now for the first time she wondered if losing Charlotte was one of the reasons Mum tended to be so overprotective. But she also knew that Mum wasn't being particularly overprotective tonight and that any of her friends' mothers would have reacted the same way if their child had disappeared from the house like that in the middle of the night. She ought to have left a note explaining where she had gone, she realized, only she wasn't sure that would have done much good, since none of her family was very likely to believe that she had been invited to a fairy party.

'I'm sorry, Mum,' Maddie said in a small voice. 'I know I shouldn't have left the house without telling you, but I just *really* wanted to go to the party in the fairy grove, like you and Aunt Rachel did.'

Mum sniffed. 'I knew I shouldn't have told you about that.'

'At least she took her inhaler with her,' Grandpa said, spotting it poking out of Maddie's pocket.

'And a whole lot of sweets by the look of it,' Grandma added, peering into the bag Maddie had put down on the table. 'She certainly wouldn't have starved if she'd got lost in the woods.'

'They're not for me. They're for the fairies,' Maddie said. 'Fairies really like chocolate, you see.'

'I think we've heard enough about fairies for one night,' Grandma said, pushing back

her chair and letting out a loud yawn. 'I reckon it's high time we all went back to bed, don't you?'

The next morning Mum said she was going to walk to the village with Milo, and she asked Maddie if she wanted to come too. Maddie had already told Milo everything that had happened the previous night and he had listened with his ears pricked up. Now, as she agreed to go with Mum, she gave Milo a meaningful look to remind him that they must both keep a lookout for the missing fairies while they were outside.

The road to the village didn't have a pavement so they had to walk on the grass verge. Luckily there were hardly any cars, although at one point they had to stand right back against the hedge to let a big open-backed truck pass them. It was heaped full of green plastic rubbish bags and Mum said it was collecting garden waste.

Mum clearly wanted to talk to Maddie again about the previous night. 'Just because we're in the country, it doesn't mean you can behave differently to how you would at home,' she told her firmly. 'I'm sorry if I gave you the impression that what Rachel and I did as children was a bit of a joke. It was actually very wrong of us, and I want you to promise me you'll never leave the house in the night like that ever again.'

Maddie sighed. 'OK, I promise.' Then she added, 'But I wish you believed in fairies, Mum.'

When they reached the village, the truck that had passed them earlier was parked across the road from the post office while the driver collected some bags of garden refuse from one of the houses nearby. The

people who lived in that house must have been doing a lot of gardening because there were lots of bags.

As they passed the truck Milo stopped abruptly and started barking.

'Shh, Milo!' Mum said sharply.

Maddie, who was holding his lead, gave it a little tug but Milo still refused to budge. He started to jump up as if he wanted to leap right into the back of the truck. 'What is it, Milo?' Maddie asked him.

'He must have smelt something interesting in those sacks of rubbish,' Mum said, taking the lead from Maddie to drag him away.

'Help! Oh, please help me!' a little voice suddenly called out. Then came the sound of tiny sobs, which seemed to be coming from the back of the truck.

'Wait, Mum!' Maddie stopped where she

was as Mum crossed the road to the post office.

The truck driver was walking down the drive with the last few garden bags, which he hurled into the back along with the others.

'WAIT!' Maddie yelled out as he went to get in the front to drive off.

'MADDIE!' Mum was calling to her impatiently from across the road.

The driver turned to look at Maddie enquiringly, and suddenly she didn't know what to say. He was going to think she was crazy if she told him she thought there was a fairy inside one of his rubbish bags.

'Better move away from the truck, love!' he told her loudly when she didn't speak. 'I'm about to pull off!'

Maddie froze as she watched him get inside and slam the door.

Immediately a muffled cry sounded again. 'Help!' It was definitely a fairy and Maddie was almost sure it was a fairy voice she had heard before. But before she could do anything else the truck's engine had started and it was pulling away.

Mum had walked back across the road to fetch her by this time and Milo was straining at his lead and yapping madly as if he wanted to race after the truck.

'Mum, there's a fairy trapped inside one of those bags!' Maddie cried out.

'Maddie, will you please stop all this nonsense about fairies?' Mum said sharply. 'Or I'm going to get really cross!'

Maddie was the one who felt cross as she waited in the post office for Mum to buy some stamps. There had definitely been a fairy inside that truck and it might have

been one of the ones who had gone missing. Maddie knew she had to rescue her – but *how*?

'Mum, do you know where that truck takes all the garden rubbish when it's been collected?' she asked. But her mother was talking to the lady who ran the post office and didn't reply.

An old lady who had come into the shop a few minutes after them looked up from the packets of envelopes she had been inspecting. 'I expect they burn it,' she told Maddie.

'*Burn* it?'

'Well, that's what I do with *my* garden rubbish. But if you really want to know, why don't you ask Jack? He's the driver. He usually stops at the cafe round the corner to have his lunch about now. They sell nice ice creams in that cafe too. Maybe your mum'll take you there – if she ever stops her chattering.'

That's when Maddie realized the lady was only looking at the envelopes to fill her time while she waited for Mum to move away from the post-office counter.

'Mum, you're holding up the queue,' she whispered, tugging at her mum's arm.

Mum turned and saw the old lady waiting behind them and immediately started to apologize.

As they left the shop together, Maddie asked, 'Mum, please can we go and get an ice cream in the cafe before we go home?'

Mum looked at her watch. 'I guess so. Come on then.'

When they turned the corner into the next street Maddie spotted the truck straight away, parked further up the road, where there was plenty of room for other

cars to get by. The truck driver was sitting in the cafe at a table by the window, waiting for his food. Jack wasn't too unfriendly-looking, Maddie thought, although he did have very bushy eyebrows.

While Mum was at the counter ordering an ice cream for Maddie and a cup of tea for herself, Maddie tied Milo to a table leg and watched the waitress take Jack a large fry-up. As soon as the waitress had gone, Maddie went over to Jack's table and asked, 'Excuse me, but what do you *do* with all that garden rubbish after you've collected it?'

'Beg pardon,' Jack said, cupping his ear.

Maddie had to repeat her question more loudly – which made her mum turn round and look at them.

'I take it to the dump,' Jack told her, through a mouthful of baked beans. 'Then

it gets recycled. Interested in waste disposal, are you?'

'Maddie, sit down at our table and stop pestering people,' Mum called over from the counter. She never liked it when Maddie was too friendly with strangers.

Luckily, at that moment Mum's mobile phone rang. She fished it out of her bag and Maddie guessed that it was Dad and that he wanted to talk to Mum about Maddie's birthday present. Maddie had asked for a bicycle, but Mum didn't want her to have one because she thought riding bicycles, especially in the street, was too dangerous. Maddie had begged her dad to get Mum to change her mind – and judging from Mum's side of the conversation that was what he was trying to do now. 'But you know how I feel about that,' Mum was saying into the phone as she came over and gave Maddie her ice-cream cone, then went back to pick up her cup of tea from the counter. 'Look, she's here with me now. I can't really talk. Wait a moment while I take the phone outside.'

Maddie quickly saw her chance. 'It's OK, Mum. You sit down and drink your tea. I'll take my ice cream outside.'

'Are you sure?'

Maddie nodded.

'Well, don't go far. Stay on the pavement in front of the cafe.'

Maddie promised, as Mum sat down to continue her talk with Dad.

Jack seemed to be eating his lunch very quickly so Maddie knew she had to hurry. She left the cafe and ran along the pavement to reach the truck, climbing up on to the metal step at the back to see over the side. 'Hello!' she called out. 'Is anyone in here?'

A muffled voice immediately came back to her. 'Yes! *I* am! Oh, please help me!'

'Are you a fairy?'

'Yes. I'm trapped inside the green rubbish bag. Can you get me out?'

Maddie looked at all the identical green bags and asked, '*Which* green rubbish bag?'

'*This* one!' The little voice was so muffled that Maddie guessed the fairy must be in one of the bags near the bottom of the pile.

She knew she would need to climb into the back of the truck to get to the bags, which meant unfastening the bolts that let the truck's back section flip down. She had just managed to tug back the second bolt when an angry voice behind her made her jump.

'*Just what do you think you're doing with my truck, young lady?*'

5

The truck's driver – Jack – had a dribble of egg yolk on his chin. Maddie did her best not to stare at it as she said in a small voice, 'I'm sorry but I . . . I thought I heard someone shouting from inside your truck.'

'Stop mumbling, can't you?' he grunted. 'I can't hear a word you're saying. And get down from there before you do yourself an injury!' He reached up to help her off the metal runner, but as she moved away the flap fell down and several bags of rubbish immediately toppled out after her.

'Now look what you've done!' Jack growled, pulling her out of the way of the tumbling bags.

As Jack started to lift the flap back into position Maddie saw her last chance to rescue the fairy slipping away. And for some reason she decided to blurt out the truth.

'But there's a *fairy* in one of those bags!' she shouted (at the top of her voice so Jack couldn't accuse her of mumbling).

To her surprise Jack instantly stopped what he was doing. 'A *fairy*? Well, why didn't you say so before?'

Maddie gaped at him.

'Mind you, I've never known one end up in the garden rubbish,' Jack continued, shaking his head. 'Normally they'd fly away the second they saw a gardener coming. Oh well, I suppose we'd better find her then, hadn't we?'

As he started to unload bags from his truck Maddie said, 'I didn't think you'd believe in fairies.'

'Eh?' He cupped his hand against his ear again.

'I said, I didn't think you'd believe in fairies!' Maddie repeated at the top of her voice.

He chuckled. 'Because I'm old enough to know better, you mean? It's true that I'm a little bit deaf now, which makes it difficult for me to hear their tiny voices, but I still spot them in the woods from time to time.'

Maddie suddenly heard an indignant cry coming from the bag Jack had just pulled down from the truck. 'Don't bump me!'

'She's in that one!' Maddie said, pointing at it.

Jack struggled to untie the bag – which

had been fastened very tightly with a triple knot – and tipped the contents out on to the pavement. Just then Maddie heard Milo barking and she looked up to see her mother waving at her impatiently from along the road.

'What are you doing there, Maddie?' her mother yelled. 'Come here at once!'

'There she is!' Jack said, glimpsing a red petal dress under a pile of leaves.

Maddie saw it too. 'Poppy!' she exclaimed excitedly.

'You'd better help her out of there,' Jack said. 'I'll go and speak to your mum.'

'Mum doesn't believe in fairies,' Maddie warned him, but he didn't seem to hear her.

As Jack walked off, Maddie helped Poppy out from all the leaves and grass cuttings. The fairy looked exhausted. One of the petals of

her skirt had been ripped and another had
come right off. There were bits of grass in
her hair – which was horribly tangled – and
her face was muddy and streaked with tears.
Her single wing was flattened against her
back.

'What happened to you? Where are the
others?' Maddie burst out.

'I don't know,' Poppy replied,
starting to shiver as she saw
Jack talking to Maddie's
mother in the
distance. 'I think that's
him – the man who
captured us!'

'Who? Jack?'
Maddie was
surprised.

'I don't
know

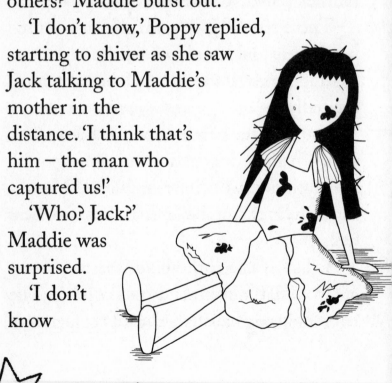

his name, but you've got to hide me. Quick! Let me climb into your pocket.' So Maddie quickly helped Poppy into the pocket of her cardigan.

Just then her mother came hurrying along the pavement towards her, with Jack following behind, shaking his head in an irritated manner. Milo started yapping again.

'Maddie, I'm very cross with you,' Mum said as soon as she reached her. 'I've told you before not to speak to strangers – and that includes ones who tell you stories about fairies!'

'But Jack's *not* telling me stories,' Maddie said. '*I* was the one who told *him* there was a fairy in his truck!'

'Really?' Mum turned to glare at Jack again. 'Well, he's gone a bit far in the way of humouring you, as far as I'm concerned!'

'He's *not* humouring me,' Maddie protested. 'Look!' She pulled her pocket wide open for her mother to look inside, but of course it was hopeless. Mum didn't believe in fairies so she couldn't see anything except Maddie's inhaler.

Jack leaned over to look in Maddie's pocket and gave Poppy a little wave, which seemed to annoy Mum even more.

'Come on, Maddie. We're going home,' Mum said, giving Jack a disapproving glare as she took Maddie's hand to march her away along the road.

Inside Maddie's pocket, Poppy was starting to relax. 'It wasn't Jack who kidnapped me,' she said. 'That old man had a different face.'

Jack stood looking after them, shaking his head and tutting. In his opinion, it was a great shame that so few adults believed in fairies. Then he slowly began to load up his truck with all the bags that were on the pavement, ready to take them off to the local dump.

'She's completely obsessed with all this fairy nonsense,' Maddie heard her mother telling her grandparents after they arrived home. Maddie was on her way up to her room, but she made sure she paused at the bottom of the stairs to listen to what the grown-ups were saying about her.

'She's at that age,' Grandma said. 'I wouldn't worry about it. Our Rachel was just the same.'

'*You* were probably the exception rather than the rule, *not* to ever believe in fairies,' Grandpa added. There was a chuckle in his voice as he asked, 'Did she really get Jack to unload his whole truck?'

'She picked the right person there,' Grandma said. 'Jack's whole family is completely eccentric. I told him the other day he should go to the doctor and get his hearing checked, but apparently his mother – who has to be ninety, at least – is brewing him up some ancient herbal remedy to improve his hearing instead. And it's a remedy recommended by the little folk, no less.'

'You shouldn't knock the old remedies,' Grandpa chided her. 'Some of them are just the ticket – though I don't know about the little folk having anything to do with them.'

'Well, *I* reckon all he needs is to get his ears syringed,' Grandma continued. 'When you had yours done last year it was truly incredible the amount of wax that came out of them.'

Mum laughed and sounded much more relaxed, so Maddie left the grown-ups talking and continued up the stairs. Poppy was getting fidgety inside her pocket, and as soon as they reached her bedroom Maddie placed her on the bed. There the fairy flung herself down on her back, stretched her arms out behind her and gave a huge sigh of relief.

'Queen Flora is ever so worried about you,' Maddie told her. She explained how she had met the fairy queen the previous night when she had tried to go to the party. 'Tell me what happened, Poppy! And where are Daisy and Primrose?'

Poppy sat up and began to relate the events of the previous day. 'It was horrible,' she said. 'We didn't know what had happened at first. We flew up to have a rest on our favourite branch and as soon as our feet

touched it we realized it was sticky, *so* sticky we couldn't lift our feet off it again. Then we all reached down to try and wipe the sticky stuff off our feet – and our hands got stuck too. It was just awful and we guessed it was bird-lime, so we called out for help. None of us had any fairy dust left because we'd used it all up making your arrows. Otherwise we could have used that to unstick ourselves.'

'Queen Flora *said* it was bird-lime!' Maddie exclaimed.

'Yes, well, before any other fairy could hear us, an old man came along. He could obviously see us and at first we thought he was going to help us. But he snapped the branch right off and shoved it – and us – into a bag on his back! After that we couldn't see anything so we couldn't even tell where he was taking us. Finally we got to wherever it was – his house, I think – and he opened the bag and took us out. He put us all in a big white sink to wash off the bird-lime from our feet and hands, and he seemed to know all about fairies because he checked all our pockets to make sure we weren't carrying any fairy dust or anything else that might help us escape. But as he was washing *my* feet he realized I only had one wing. That seemed to make him cross, and instead of putting me in a cage along with Daisy and Primrose he took me outside and put me in that bag with all the garden rubbish.'

'Poppy, that's terrible!' Maddie exclaimed. She didn't know what was more terrible – the fact that Poppy and the others had been kidnapped in the first place, or the fact that Poppy had been thrown away on account of only having one wing.

'I guess for once in my life being a freak

has worked in my favour,' Poppy said jokily.

'Don't say that,' Maddie snapped. 'You're not a freak and you shouldn't say that, even as a joke.'

'Well, what else do you call a fairy who's only got one wing?' Poppy said. 'I'm not exactly normal, am I?'

'Just because you've got something wrong with your body doesn't make you a freak,' Maddie said firmly.

Poppy sighed. 'If you say so.' She was looking around Maddie's bedroom. 'Do you have this room all to yourself then? In fairyland there are so many of us that we all have to share.'

'Yes – but it's only mine while I'm staying with Grandma and Grandpa. My real bedroom is at home.'

'Do you have any brothers or sisters?'

'No.' Maddie paused. 'I did have a twin sister, but she died soon after we were born.'

'That's a shame. I expect you'd have liked a sister, wouldn't you?'

Maddie nodded. 'I often wonder what she'd have been like. I reckon we'd have done everything together.'

'Queen Flora says that human children are very special,' Poppy said. 'She says there's so much potential in every human child that it's no wonder that whenever one dies . . .' She broke off suddenly, as if she thought she might have said too much, and quickly changed the subject. 'What's that thing you carry in your pocket? It's not very comfortable to sit on.'

'Oh, that's just my inhaler. It's a sort of spray with medicine inside that I have to use sometimes because of my asthma.'

'What's asthma?' Poppy asked curiously.

'It's a sort of illness that makes you get all wheezy and breathless. Most of the time I'm perfectly all right though. But listen, Poppy, we have to try and find Daisy and Primrose before anything bad happens to them.'

'I know, but *how* are we going to find them? That old man's house could be anywhere.'

'Well, it's got to be one of the houses that Jack collects garden rubbish from, which means it's got to be somewhere near here. Can you remember *anything* about him – or about his house?'

'I didn't see his house except the inside of that big white sink. And I didn't notice much about him, except that he had a very unfriendly face.'

'Well, was he tall or short? Was he thin

or fat? What colour hair did he have? What was he wearing?' Maddie prompted.

Poppy frowned as if she was trying hard to remember. 'The trouble is, *all* humans look tall if you're a fairy, and I couldn't see his hair because he was wearing a hat. He wasn't really thin or fat – somewhere in between. His clothes were very ordinary, as far as I remember.'

'Did he speak to you at all?'

'Only once. He was very rude,' Poppy remembered now. 'When he was dumping me in the rubbish bag he said that he only collected *perfect* specimens.'

Maddie stared at her. 'He said that? That he *collected* things?'

Poppy nodded. 'Perfect specimens – that's what he said.'

'Was he carrying a butterfly net?'

'I didn't see one.'

'Well, did you see any butterflies inside his house? Dead ones, I mean – in glass cases?'

Poppy shook her head. 'I told you. All I saw was the inside of the sink.'

'Listen, Poppy, I think I know who this old man might be. I think it might be someone called Horace Hatter, who went to school with my grandfather.' Maddie told Poppy how they had seen Mr Hatter in the woods, and how her grandfather had told her that Horace was obsessed with collecting things. 'He used to collect butterflies – but what if he's moved on to fairies?'

Poppy looked appalled. 'Do you really think someone would collect *us*?'

'I bet Horace would! But don't worry. If it *is* him, we can go to his house straight away and rescue Primrose and Daisy.'

'Do you know where he lives then?'

'No – but my grandpa does. Come on! Let's go and ask him!'

6

As she rushed to the door she realized that Poppy wasn't following. 'Sorry,' she said. 'I forgot you can't fly. You can sit inside my pocket again if you like.'

'I'd rather sit on your shoulder,' Poppy replied. 'Then I can see what's happening. None of your family believes in fairies, do they?'

'No,' Maddie said.

'Good. That means they won't be able to see *me*.'

Maddie lifted Poppy up on to her right

shoulder. 'I'm just a bit worried you might fall off,' she said.

'Oh, but I won't! See, I can hold on to your hair really tightly.'

Maddie wasn't sure she liked the sound of that but since Poppy was already clutching her hair and she couldn't even feel it, she guessed it was OK.

'Fairies don't weigh anything you see,' Poppy explained to her. 'I could swing from your hair or climb up it as if I was climbing up a rope, and you wouldn't feel a thing! Shall I show you?'

'No, thanks,' Maddie said quickly, turning to look in the mirror to check what Poppy was doing. Poppy was standing on one leg, pointing the other one outwards like a ballet dancer and steadying herself by holding on to Maddie's ear lobe. 'Stop mucking about, Poppy!' she said, but she couldn't help giggling because it did look pretty funny.

They went downstairs and found Maddie's grandfather in the back garden examining his roses for greenfly. Milo was in the garden too and Poppy asked Maddie to put her down on the ground so she could go and speak to him.

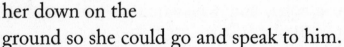

'I'll have to spray these roses again – the little pests are all over them,' Grandpa grunted to Maddie as she joined him.

'Tell him I'll have a word with those greenfly if he wants and he won't need to spray them,' Poppy called out.

But somehow Maddie didn't think her

grandfather would believe her if she told him that.

'Grandpa,' she began slowly, 'you know how you told me Mr Hatter has a really big butterfly collection?'

'Yes, sweetheart. A lot of people used to collect butterflies in the old days, I'm afraid.'

'It's just that I'd like to see it.'

Grandpa looked at her in surprise. 'I thought you didn't approve of butterflies being captured?'

'Well...' Maddie quickly tried to think up something to say that wasn't an absolute lie. 'I certainly don't approve of him capturing any *more* butterflies, but... but... if they're already dead ...'

'I didn't know you were so interested in butterflies,' Grandpa said, staring at her.

'Well, I wasn't until ... until ...' She

looked over at Poppy for help, but the fairy wasn't looking in her direction. Instead Poppy was balanced on Milo's head, holding up one of the dog's floppy ears while she whispered into it.

Suddenly Maddie's eyes fell on Grandpa's library book that was lying face down on the garden table. '... Until I got a book out of the library that's all about butterflies and it's really interesting,' she blurted.

'Really? Wouldn't you rather go looking for live ones in the woods then?'

'Yes, but ... but I'd just really like to see if Mr Hatter's got the same ones that are in my book,' Maddie said.

'Hmm ... I'd like to see this book,' Grandpa said, going back to his roses.

'Well ...' Maddie was stuck now.

Fortunately Poppy had started to pay attention to their conversation. 'Tell him it's

upstairs and you'll show it to him later,' she hissed as Milo gave her a ride back across the garden.

So Maddie said that — although she didn't have a clue how she was actually going to find a book on butterflies at such short notice. Luckily Grandpa was too preoccupied with his greenfly to question her any further.

'Poppy, *where* am I going to get a book

on butterflies?' Maddie burst out as soon as they were back in her room again.

'I don't know, but I think I'd better go and let Queen Flora know what's happened.'

'When I met Queen Flora in the woods last night she said she was going to a meeting of the Fairy High Council in Scotland,' Maddie told her. 'She said she was going to seal off the entrance to fairyland until she got back.'

'Oh,' Poppy exclaimed, sounding disappointed. 'That means *I* can't get back into fairyland yet either. If she's gone to Scotland she must have flown there at sunrise this morning and she won't be back until sunset tonight. Flower fairies have to travel at sunset and sunrise if they want to get anywhere instantly. We're not like book fairies who can travel wherever they

want to *whenever* they want to, through
their entry-books.'

'*Book* fairies?' Maddie queried in
astonishment.

'Yes. Haven't you heard of them?'

Maddie shook her head.

'Oh, there are many more types of fairy
than just us,' Poppy told her. 'The most
common kinds are flower fairies, book
fairies, tooth fairies and dream fairies.'

'I know about flower fairies and tooth
fairies,' Maddie said, 'but I've never heard
of book fairies or dream fairies before.'

'You have to sleep in a magic bed to meet
a dream fairy,' Poppy explained, 'and book
fairies live in Book-fairy Land, but they
visit here quite a lot through their entry-
books.'

'What's an entry-book?' Maddie asked,
completely fascinated now.

91

'It's a magic book that you find in a library. It acts as a passageway between here and Book-fairy Land. You usually find them in the reference section or on a top shelf where humans can't reach them very easily.'

Maddie was about to ask more questions when Poppy's face suddenly lit up. 'I've got an idea,' she said. 'It's Thursday today, isn't it? Well, on Thursday afternoons the mobile library always comes to this village. I know because there's an entry-book inside it and sometimes my friend Opal comes through it to meet me. Opal's a book fairy. I met her when she flew off to explore the village one Thursday and the mobile library left before she got back. She had to wait a whole week until she could go home again, but luckily she guessed there would be flower fairies in the woods so she came and stayed with us while she was waiting.'

'Wow!' Maddie could hardly believe all the new things she was learning about fairies. 'Do you think Opal will be there today?'

'I don't know, but let's go there now. There's bound to be a book on butterflies that you can take to show your grandfather.'

'But I'm not allowed to go into the village on my own,' Maddie told her.

'Get your mother to come with us then.'

'We've only just come back from the village. I don't think she'll want to go again right now.'

'Well, ask your grandmother or your grandfather,' Poppy said impatiently.

'I can't get out a book on butterflies when Grandpa's there, can I?' Maddie sighed. 'I could ask Grandma, I suppose.'

When Maddie went downstairs she found Grandma doing some baking and

Mum sitting on a stool in the kitchen chatting to her. 'I need to go into the village again,' she told them. 'I want to get a book from the mobile library.'

'I didn't know you knew about our mobile library, Maddie,' Grandma said.

'Oh, I've just seen it here before on a Thursday,' Maddie mumbled. 'Could I borrow your library card, Grandma?'

'Of course. It's in the bureau if you want to use it.'

'You brought lots of books with you from home, Maddie,' Mum said. 'Why do you need to get more from the library?'

'I just want to,' Maddie muttered.

'Well, I really don't feel like walking into the village again this afternoon, and Grandma and Grandpa are both busy,' Mum said firmly.

Just then Poppy jumped down from

Maddie's shoulder on to the kitchen table. The next moment Grandma's eggs, which had been sitting in their cardboard carton waiting to be used in the cake mix, went tumbling down on to the stone kitchen floor.

'Oh, goodness!' Grandma cried out. The lid of the carton had been open and all of the eggs had fallen out and smashed. Now there was yolk and egg white and bits of broken shell all over the floor.

'How on earth did that happen?' Mum exclaimed.

Maddie was staring at Poppy, who was rubbing her hands together in satisfaction as she stood beside Grandma's mixing bowl.

'I'll *have* to go to the village now to get some more,' Grandma said.

'Maddie ...' Mum began suspiciously, but Grandma interrupted her.

'You can't blame her. She wasn't standing anywhere near those eggs. I don't know how it happened. I must have pushed something against them without realizing, I suppose.'

'Well, let me go and get the eggs for you.'

'No, no. You stay here and clean this lot up. I've been in all morning. A bit of fresh air will do me good. Come on, Maddie. You can come to the village with me and we can stop at the library if you like.'

So Maddie and her grandmother set off for the village with Poppy riding on Maddie's shoulder, complaining the whole way about what a slow method of travelling this was compared to flying along with the other fairies.

'Your grandfather had better hurry up and take you to see this Horace Hatter after this,' Poppy said impatiently. 'And Milo had better remember what to do when we get there.'

'*Milo's* got to do something?'

'Yes – I told him all about it while we were in the garden. As soon as we get to Horace's house you must let him off his lead, OK?'

'OK,' Maddie said. 'But I hope you haven't asked him to do anything silly.'

They soon arrived at the village and Grandma showed Maddie where the mobile library was. It was quite a small van, which was sitting in front of the post office with its back doors open. There was nobody inside it because the librarian was in the post office talking to the lady behind the counter.

'Go in and choose what book you want,' Grandma told her. 'I'll go and get my eggs and come back for you.'

As Maddie stepped inside the van, she said, 'OK, Poppy, let's look under B for Butterflies.'

Together they searched the shelves under B and then under N for Nature. But there were no books on butterflies. Just as Maddie was getting desperate Poppy shrieked excitedly, 'Look – the entry-book is glowing! I can never remember which one it is until it starts doing that!'

She was pointing at a large book on the top shelf, which was sparkling as they watched it. Maddie could hardly believe her eyes as it slid out from its shelf all by itself and hovered in the air for a few moments. Then the book opened and the page it had opened at began to glow gold. A beam of light suddenly shot out from the book and something white came whizzing towards them in the beam, getting bigger and bigger

as it got closer, until suddenly a fairy was there in front of them.

'Opal!' Poppy shrieked, leaping off Maddie's shoulder.

'Poppy!' Opal shrieked back, flying forward to grab Poppy by both arms before she could fall to the ground.

Opal was a very pretty fairy with her hair in long golden bunches. Her dress was

a whitish colour with bluish-green flecks in it, which seemed to sparkle as she moved about. Poppy quickly introduced her to Maddie and told her why they were there. But she had hardly finished speaking when Opal burst out, 'One of *our* fairies has gone missing too. Her name's Emerald and I was just coming to look for her. She went missing from the mobile library last week when it came to this village.'

'I hope she hasn't been kidnapped along with Primrose and Daisy,' Poppy said.

'Why would anyone want to kidnap her?' Opal exclaimed.

'There's a man who lives here who likes to collect things,' Maddie told her, 'and I think he might have started collecting fairies. If he has, then I guess he's probably interested in collecting different *types* of fairies.'

Opal looked horrified. 'Our fairy queen

was called to a Fairy High Council meeting in Scotland early this morning. Is this what it's about?'

'Yes. Queen Flora has gone there too,' Poppy explained. 'Maybe you could go there and tell her and all the other fairy queens that we know who the kidnapper is. There's bound to be a library near to where they're having their meeting, isn't there?' She quickly turned to Maddie and said, 'It's like I told you – book fairies can travel to other libraries instantly if there's an entry-book there.'

Opal was nodding. 'I'll go there as soon as I've had a look outside for Emerald. After all, she might not have been kidnapped. She might just have got lost.'

'There's no time to lose,' Poppy said. 'I'll go and look for Emerald – but *you* have to go straight to Scotland, Opal.'

101

'Well, all right then,' Opal agreed. 'Emerald's got blonde hair and a bright green dress and she's very nervous around humans so you probably shouldn't take Maddie when you go looking for her. I'll go back through the entry-book now and see what I can do. You never know. Our fairy queen might even bring all the other fairy queens back through this entry-book with her when she hears what's happened.'

As she spoke, the entry-book, which had continued to sparkle as they talked, suddenly produced another beam of light. 'I'll see you in a little while,' Opal said, flying into the light beam and disappearing inside it.

Maddie just stared at the book open-mouthed.

Poppy, who had been left standing on the shelf, said, 'Thank goodness for that. When Queen Flora and the other fairy queens

come back they'll know what to do, and they'll bring lots of fairy dust with them.'

'Are you going to look for Emerald now?' Maddie asked.

'Yes. You'd better stay here. I'll ask a bird to give me a ride. You get a much better view from the air.'

'I thought you weren't allowed to go for rides on birds in case you fell off.'

'I'm not going to fall off – anyway, this is an emergency!'

Maddie took Poppy outside and placed her on the ground, where she immediately started to chirp at a thrush who was pecking at the earth in a nearby garden. The thrush flew over to her and Poppy spoke to it in chirps and twitters. Soon the fairy was climbing aboard the bird's back.

'Be careful, won't you?' Maddie said anxiously, because Poppy was so busy chattering to the bird in its own language that she didn't look like she was concentrating very hard on holding on.

'Don't fuss!' Poppy snapped, giving her a little glare as the thrush took off. 'I'll meet you back at the house in a little while, and we can go and visit Horace together.'

Maddie stepped back into the library van and spent another few minutes looking in vain for a book about butterflies. Suddenly a figure appeared in the doorway and she turned her head, expecting to see the librarian. But instead she gasped in shock as she saw that the person who had stepped into the back of the van was Horace Hatter himself.

7

Mr Hatter was staring at Maddie and he seemed about to say something when a plump, cheerful lady appeared behind him, who Maddie realized must be the librarian.

'Hello, Mr Hatter. Come to choose another book? How was the one I ordered in for you?'

'Too many pictures, not enough facts,' Horace grunted, and it was then that Maddie noticed the large hardback book he was holding. It had a picture of a big red

butterfly on the cover. He handed it to the librarian.

'Hello, dear. Can I help you?' the librarian said to Maddie.

Maddie thought very quickly. 'I'd like to borrow that book, please,' she said, pointing at the one Horace had just handed in.

'You like butterflies too, do you?' The lady smiled at her. 'Have you got your ticket?'

Maddie handed it to her. 'It's my grandma's, but she says I can use it.'

Behind them Horace was reaching up to take a book down from the shelf and, to Maddie's horror, she saw that the book he had picked out was the magic entry-book.

'You can't take that!' Maddie blurted before she could stop herself.

Horace and the librarian stared at her in surprise. Now that the entry-book had stopped glowing it looked just like any other book.

'Mr Hatter can choose whichever one he likes, dear,' the librarian said briskly.

Horace stepped over to her with the entry-book in his hand. 'Here's my card,' he muttered.

'Thank you, dear. Just let me scan the barcode . . .'

Horace held it up for her to scan, and quickly left.

'Here's your book,' the librarian said, handing Maddie the book on butterflies.

Maddie rushed outside, knowing that she had to find Poppy and get Grandpa to take them to Horace Hatter's house straight away. She hurried to the village store, where Grandma was chatting to her friend, Wilma, who worked there. There were some plastic bags on the counter and

Maddie quickly took one and slipped her book inside. She didn't want to broadcast the fact that she had only just acquired a book on butterflies.

'Have you got your eggs, Grandma?' Maddie asked.

Grandma nodded and smiled at her. 'Did you find a good book?'

'Yes.'

'What did you get?'

'Oh ... it's just a book about ... about things you get in the countryside ...' Maddie said vaguely. 'I suppose we'd better get back so you can finish your baking, hadn't we?' she added, taking a hopeful step towards the door.

Grandma laughed. 'What she means is that she wants me to stop my gossiping and get a move on,' she told Wilma.

They were only halfway home when

they met Grandpa walking along the road towards them with Milo.

'Is everything all right?' Grandma asked him immediately.

'Of course. I just fancied stretching my legs, that's all – thought I'd come and meet you. I just passed Horace Hatter. He'd been to the library too. Miserable-looking book he'd got under his arm.'

'Poor Horace,' Grandma said. 'He came into the shop today on his way to the library. I was talking to Wilma and we were just saying afterwards that he must get very lonely living in that big old house all on his own. He never has anyone to stay as far as I know, and Wilma says he's always on his own whenever she sees him.'

'If you ask me, Horace likes being on his own,' Grandpa grunted. 'He never mixed as a boy either, as far as I remember,

unless he was trying to swap one of his stamps.'

'He must have had a very lonely life,' Grandma said.

'I asked Grandpa if he'd take me to see Mr Hatter's butterfly collection,' Maddie put in quickly.

'Well, you know, that's not a bad idea,' Grandma said. 'It wouldn't hurt at all for him to have a bit of company. I reckon you *should* take her,' she told Grandpa firmly.

'If *you're* so worried about him all of a sudden, why don't *you* take Maddie to visit him?' Grandpa retorted.

'Because *you're* the one who knows him best. Anyway, I've got to get on. I've got my cake to bake – unless you don't want cake this week. You can take Maddie to see Horace after you've walked me home.

Stretch your legs over to *his* house, why don't you?'

Grandpa sighed. 'We can go and see Horace if you really want to, Maddie. But I'm warning you now – don't expect a warm welcome when we get there.'

'Don't worry, Grandpa – I'm not expecting that,' Maddie said.

They walked back with Grandma as far as their own house where Maddie looked in the garden for any sign of Poppy. She also made an excuse to go inside and up to her bedroom to see if Poppy was there, but she wasn't. Maddie guessed she must still be out looking for the missing book fairy.

'Come on, Maddie. It's now or never as far as I'm concerned,' Grandpa shouted to her. 'And why don't you bring that butterfly book you were talking about?'

Maddie knew that she was just going to

have to do this without Poppy, and she only hoped that Milo would remember whatever it was *he* was meant to be doing.

Soon Maddie was following Grandpa up the road towards Mr Hatter's house, holding Milo on the lead in case a car came past.

'Horace might not even open the door to us,' Grandpa warned her.

Maddie frowned. She was worried about that, but she guessed she would just have to face that problem when she came to it.

They soon arrived at a very large old house set back from the road that didn't look in a very good state of repair.

'Believe it or not, Horace has lived in this place all his life,' Grandpa told her. 'It used to belong to his parents and he's lived here on his own ever since they died.'

They opened the front gate and Maddie

remembered what Poppy had told her and quickly bent down to unclip Milo's lead.

As they walked up to the front porch, they noticed that all the curtains were drawn across. 'He told me once that he likes a dark house,' Grandpa said. 'Said it preserves his specimens better or something.' He shook his head as if he thought Horace was very strange indeed.

They had to ring the bell twice before the door opened a short way and Horace peered at them through the gap. 'Yes?' he grunted.

Grandpa cheerfully explained that Maddie was very interested in seeing his butterfly collection.

'It's a private collection ... it's not for children to gawp at,' Horace answered curtly, beginning to close the door again.

Milo, who had been sniffing a plant in

the garden, seemed to spring into action. He ran at top speed towards Maddie and Grandpa, brushing past their legs and Horace's to shoot through the front door and into the house.

Horace whirled round and shouted at him, and Grandpa called out his name very sharply too, but Milo had already found the staircase and was bounding up it. Horace rushed into the house after him, leaving the front door open, and Maddie quickly stepped inside.

Grandpa followed her. He had stopped calling for Milo to come back, she noticed, and instead he gave her a wink. 'I can't say I wanted to come and visit Horace in the first place, but seeing as I'm here . . .'

As Horace started to climb the stairs after Milo, Maddie and Grandpa stood in the large dark hallway and had a good look round.

'When I was a boy I always wanted to get a peek inside this place,' Grandpa whispered, 'but Horace never invited anybody in.'

The hall had a patterned carpet and the walls were covered with old-fashioned flowery wallpaper that was peeling a bit in places. There were four doors leading off from the hall and three of them were open. Maddie put the butterfly book she had brought with her on the hall table and followed Grandpa – who was leading the way enthusiastically now – into the nearest room. She did a double take when she saw inside it. All over the walls were cases and cases of butterflies. Lined up along the mantelpiece and on shelf units on either side of it were rows of stuffed birds and animals with staring glass eyes, and on the

coffee table there was a large glass case displaying dead beetles.

Leaving Grandpa to look around, Maddie slipped out into the hall again and headed for the open door opposite, which led into a large dining room. There was a large dark-wood table in the centre and a matching Welsh dresser, the shelves of which were heaving with old-fashioned china crockery. There was also a huge collection of china ornaments displayed along the mantelpiece and filling two large glass cabinets on either side of the fireplace.

'When we were children Horace used to boast about how his father collected dead animals and his mother collected expensive china and how they had the biggest collections in the country,' Grandpa said, coming to join her. He walked over to the mantelpiece and began to inspect the

ornaments. 'I wonder if it's here ...' he murmured.

'You wonder if *what's* here, Grandpa?' Maddie asked him in surprise.

Grandpa lowered his voice, even though Horace was still chasing Milo about upstairs. 'When I was a boy Horace came to my house once to try and get me to swap him a stamp he particularly wanted. His mother came to collect him and noticed the one good china ornament my mother had in the front room. She took a fancy to it and asked my mother if she could buy it. My mother refused. Not long after that Horace came round again, and that evening my mother went into the front room and saw that the ornament was gone. She went to the Hatters' house to speak to Horace, but his parents wouldn't let her through the front door. She even told our local bobby, who paid them a call, but he didn't have any luck with them either.'

'What's a bobby?' Maddie asked.

Grandpa laughed. 'It's an old name for a policeman. Listen, you go and help catch Milo. I'm going to have a look through this lot to see if I can spot that piece of my mother's. Wouldn't it be funny if after all these years . . .' Grandpa's eyes had lit up like a young boy's, Maddie saw, as she went back into the hall again.

Horace was already on his way down the stairs, dragging a very yappy Milo by the collar. 'You should keep this animal on a lead,' he spluttered.

'Oh, I will,' Maddie burst out, rushing up the stairs to take Milo from Horace – and promptly letting him go again. As Milo raced back up to the top landing, Mr Hatter looked as if his face was going

to explode. Maddie darted down into the hall again, and as Horace climbed back up the stairs, she looked at the two remaining doors. The one that was open clearly led into the kitchen, so she hurried across to the door that was shut and tried the handle.

Unfortunately Milo wasn't as nimble this time. Mr Hatter caught him again straight away and kept a firm hold of his collar as he dragged him back downstairs. He reached the hall just as Maddie was opening the door (which she had half expected to be locked) and entering the room.

'HEY!' he shouted, making her jump. His face was red with anger as he used the hand that wasn't holding Milo to point towards the front door. 'Out!' he rasped. 'Get out of my house right now!'

But Maddie had already seen inside the room, and although she hadn't spotted any fairies, she *had* seen several empty birdcages.

8

Maddie stood where she was and turned bravely to face Horace. 'What are all those cages for?' she asked him.

'That's none of your business!' Horace snapped. 'Now get out!'

'Horace, can you come here a minute?' Grandpa called out from the dining room. 'I'd like to ask you about one of these ornaments.'

Horace looked startled, as if he hadn't realized that Grandpa was wandering all over his house too. He took Milo to the

front door and shoved him outside, closing the door behind him before making his way to the dining room. 'You'd better get out there and make sure he doesn't run off,' he said gruffly to Maddie.

'OK,' Maddie said, though she had no intention of doing that just yet. Anyway, Milo wouldn't run off if he knew that she and Grandpa were still inside the house.

As soon as Horace had gone into the dining room she stepped inside the room with the cages. It seemed to be another, smaller, sitting room. The birdcages were the really old-fashioned, free-standing kind you hardly ever saw nowadays. Maddie looked all round the room, but there was no sign of the missing fairies.

There was one locked cupboard and Maddie stood with her ear pressed against it, calling, 'Daisy! Primrose! Are you in there?' She held her breath for a few moments, but there was no reply.

Maddie glanced again at the cages, thinking about the butterflies on display in the glass cases in the other room. It would be far better if these cages *were* meant for the fairies, she thought, since at least that would mean Horace wasn't planning on sticking a big pin through their bodies and displaying them on a piece of card.

Maddie reminded herself that she had to look for the entry-book too. It didn't seem to be in this room, so maybe she should try the kitchen.

As she tiptoed back out into the hall again, Grandpa came striding into the hall as well, holding a rather ugly china ornament of a shepherdess in one hand. Horace was close behind him.

'Put that back!' Horace was shouting.

'I knew it was you who had stolen it!' Grandpa exclaimed.

'How dare you!'

'How dare *you*! Maddie, come on! We're going home!'

Maddie knew this was her last chance to find out if Daisy and Primrose were there. And since she couldn't think of any other way, she blurted out, 'Mr Hatter, have you stolen any *fairies*?'

Horace looked at her as if he thought she had lost her mind.

But Grandpa was clearly keen to leave now. 'Maddie, come on!' He held out his free hand for Maddie to come with him as he stepped out through the front door.

They hurried down the path with Horace shouting after them, 'You bring that back or I'll have the police on to you!'

'You do that!' Grandpa yelled back. 'I just

wish my mother was alive to see this!' And he marched off down the road clutching the ornament protectively.

Poppy was waiting in Maddie's bedroom when they got back, having been dropped off on the window ledge by the thrush. She told Maddie there had been no sign of Emerald and that none of the other birds or animals she had asked had seen her since the previous week. 'I think she must have been kidnapped too,' Poppy said gloomily.

Maddie explained how she had gone to Horace Hatter's house with Grandpa and not found anything apart from the empty birdcages. 'I wanted to wait for you to come too, Poppy, but there wasn't time.'

'That's OK. Did Milo go and look upstairs like I told him?'

'Yes – if it wasn't for him we'd never

have got into the house in the first place.'

'I'd better go and ask him what he saw,' Poppy said.

So she went and had a chat with Milo, who barked back that there had been no sign of any fairies in any of the upstairs rooms, but that there *had* been a very rude cat who didn't believe in fairies and had laughed at him when he'd asked her about them.

That evening Maddie and Poppy were both feeling very disappointed and helpless. There seemed no way of rescuing Poppy's friends since they didn't know where they were.

'We'll just have to wait for Queen Flora,' Poppy said tiredly.

'Didn't Opal say she might bring Queen Flora and the others back from Scotland through the entry-book?' Maddie asked in a worried voice. 'And if Horace has got the entry-book, doesn't that mean he'll be able to capture them too?'

'Don't worry about that,' Poppy replied. 'Entry-books don't work unless they're in a library. Queen Flora will have to travel back to the fairy grove at sunset like she normally does – and sunset won't be long now.'

Meanwhile Grandpa had dug out some old family photographs. In one of them his mother and father were standing in front of the fireplace, and just behind them on the mantelpiece was the shepherdess ornament.

'Are you sure Horace's family didn't just buy that same ornament themselves?' Grandma said.

'I know this is my mother's,' Grandpa replied. 'Look . . . see that missing ear just

there?' He pointed to the lamb that was sitting on the shepherdess's lap, and sure enough one of its ears had been chipped off. 'When I was a boy I was playing with my bat and ball inside the house and I accidently knocked it over. My mother didn't half hit the roof, I can tell you. Oh, no, you don't forget a thing like that!'

'Oh well . . .' Grandma sighed. 'But still, it was such a long time ago. If Horace goes to the police . . .'

'Oh, he won't go to the police,' Grandpa said confidently. 'He knows it's mine. He won't dare try to take it back now.' And Grandpa stayed in an exceptionally good mood for the rest of the evening.

But something was bothering Maddie. She couldn't think what it was but it was *something*. On the face of it, the fact that Horace was a known thief just made it

all the more obvious that he was the one who had stolen the fairies. But there was something about the whole thing that didn't fit together.

Upstairs in Maddie's bedroom Poppy was sitting on the window ledge looking out at the sky. 'I always forget that sunset takes forever to come in the summer time,' she complained. 'But it's nearly here now – and it's time we set off for the fairy grove. You'll have to take me there, Maddie.'

'But I can't go into the woods on my own,' Maddie protested. 'Mum won't let me.'

'Can't you sneak out without her seeing?'

Maddie shook her head. 'She'll be too worried.' She couldn't bear to upset her mother again.

'I'll just have to get another bird to give

me a ride, I suppose,' Poppy said. She went to the window and started to make a noise that was just like a bird chirping.

Maddie watched as a blackbird paused in mid-air and flew across to settle on the window ledge. Poppy cheeped at the bird who chirped something back a bit crossly. Poppy sighed loudly.

'What did she say?' Maddie asked.

'That it's dinner time and she's in the middle of feeding her babies. They're in a nest nearby and she has to go straight back to them.'

They watched the blackbird fly away. Poppy was about to start chirping again when she spotted something moving down in the garden. 'Quick!' she said. 'I think it's a squirrel. It might give me a ride if I ask it nicely.'

So Maddie carried Poppy downstairs,

through the kitchen, where her mother and grandmother were chatting as they did the dishes together, and out into the back garden. The squirrel had scurried to the far end of the garden when it heard the back door open, but it stopped when Poppy called out to it.

Maddie lifted Poppy down off her shoulder and placed her carefully on the grass. Poppy walked across to get closer to the squirrel, and when she spoke to it, the squirrel started to make urgent squeaking noises back.

'I don't believe it!' Poppy burst out. 'She says she's in the middle of feeding *her* babies too! She's about to go looking for nuts for them. And she says she can't leave them on their own for long.'

Suddenly Maddie remembered the chocolate nuts she had bought to take to

the fairy party. They were still in a paper bag in her bedroom. 'I've got lots of nuts I can give them,' she said. 'Why don't I feed her babies while she takes you to the fairy grove? Tell her I'll look after them really well until she gets back.'

Poppy relayed all this to the mother squirrel, who cocked her head to one side and inspected Maddie closely. She chattered to Poppy again and this time Poppy smiled. 'She says you can look after them as long as you stay with them the whole time and don't let anyone else touch them. She's going to fetch them for you.'

'I'll go and fetch the nuts,' Maddie said, racing back into the house.

When she got outside again the mother squirrel had reappeared with four babies, each of which was scurrying around on the lawn excitedly.

'The mother says they're very silly so you'll have to keep a firm eye on them,' Poppy said. 'It won't take her long to get to the fairy grove and back again. Squirrels can run a lot faster than a fairy can walk and she says she'll take some short cuts through the treetops.'

'Well, be careful you don't fall off,' Maddie said.

'You sound just like Queen Flora!'

'Well, I'm worried about you,' Maddie protested. 'Promise me you'll hold on really tight.'

Poppy promised, but Maddie still felt a bit worried as she watched Poppy and the squirrel disappear into the woods together.

Maddie had been sitting with the baby squirrels in her lap for several minutes when her mother came outside to join her. She was feeding them the chocolate nuts, which they seemed to find delicious, apart from the chocolate coating which they scraped off as if it was the husk.

Mum couldn't believe it when she saw the squirrels. She immediately lowered her voice to a gentle whisper so as not to scare them as she asked, 'Where did you find them?'

'At the bottom of the garden.'

'I've never seen baby squirrels as tame as this. Is their mother about?'

'Oh yes. She'll be back soon.'

Mum said she was going to get the camera, and when she got back the babies were climbing all over Maddie, swinging from her hair and tickling her nose with their little bushy tails.

Mum took some photographs and called Grandma and Grandpa outside to see the squirrels too. The sun was going down and Maddie hoped Poppy had reached the fairy grove safely.

Eventually the mother squirrel returned. Maddie saw her at the edge of the garden, and so did her young, who immediately left Maddie and scurried over to join her. Maddie's mum, who had stayed in the garden with her, sat very still watching them too. When the squirrels had gone Mum put her arm round Maddie and gave her a hug. 'What a lovely thing to happen,' she said, almost in a whisper.

Maddie nodded, scouring the edge of the woods for any sign of Poppy or the fairy queen. But they clearly hadn't returned with the squirrel.

'I'm sorry I've been a bit uptight lately,

Maddie,' Mum said suddenly. 'It's just that after you were so ill . . .'

'I understand, Mum,' Maddie replied. 'But I'm not ill now.'

Mum sighed. 'I know, Maddie. I do try not to be overprotective, but sometimes it's difficult.'

'Mum, if I was tiny like a fairy and I wanted to ride through the trees on the back of a squirrel . . . would you be worried about that?' Maddie asked suddenly, thinking about how protective of Poppy she had felt just a short while earlier.

Mum smiled. 'Ah – we're back to fairies again, are we?' She paused. 'Well, I suppose if you were a fairy you'd have wings so I wouldn't need to worry about you falling off, would I?'

'But what if I *didn't* have wings – what if

I only had *one* wing and I couldn't fly like the other fairies?'

'Well, then I'd be worried, I suppose. What a funny question!'

'It's fairy stuff, Mum. Fairies are real, you know. You just have to believe in them to get to see one.'

'I see.' Mum stood up, looking amused. 'Come on. I think it's time for bed.'

They went upstairs and as Maddie changed into her pyjamas Mum said, 'It's Friday tomorrow. One more day and then it's your birthday. Are you excited?'

Maddie nodded, though in fact she had almost forgotten about her birthday what with everything else that had been happening. That night as she lay in bed she thought about how the best birthday present of all would be if the missing fairies were found again.

Then, just as she was falling off to sleep, she realized what it was that had been niggling her about Horace Hatter. If he demanded perfection in all the things he collected – which he must do if he had rejected Poppy for only having one wing – then why had he kept that chipped shepherdess ornament all these years?

9

Maddie woke up just after midnight to find something multicoloured and sparkly flitting about her room. It was Queen Flora. 'Hello, Maddie. I wanted to come and thank you for rescuing Poppy.'

Maddie sat up in bed and rubbed her eyes. 'Is she with you? Did she get back to the fairy grove safely?'

'Yes, she did, thanks to you.'

'Have you found Daisy and Primrose yet?'

'Come out into the garden with me,

Maddie, and I will explain everything. There are a few other fairies who want to meet you.'

Maddie slipped a cardigan on over her pyjamas and followed Queen Flora down the stairs. 'Did Poppy tell you about Mr Hatter?'

'Yes. We have already been to visit him.'

'Really? It's just that I've been thinking . . .'

They had reached the garden now and the moon was out. As Maddie stepped outside she saw several fairies waiting for her. She saw Poppy straight away, sitting beside her friend Opal on the grass. Opal's dress was shimmering in the moonlight and Poppy had clearly had a wash and repaired her own dress back in Fairyland because her petal skirt was as good as new and her dark hair was sleek and shiny again.

'You'll never guess what!' Poppy said excitedly.

'It wasn't Mr Hatter who kidnapped you, was it?' Maddie said softly.

Poppy looked surprised. 'How did you know?'

'I've been thinking about it. He didn't throw away Grandpa's shepherdess just

because *that* wasn't perfect, so I'm pretty sure he wouldn't throw away a fairy with only one wing.'

'Well, you're right,' Poppy said. 'It wasn't Mr Hatter. I knew as soon as I saw his face. He *does* believe in fairies though, and he's almost as interested in us as he is in butterflies. Queen Flora spoke to him and he told us everything.'

'Everything?'

'Yes – he admitted that he was *thinking* about trying to catch a fairy in his net that day when you met him. But then he saw some fairies playing in the woods and he decided it was more interesting to watch us in our natural habitat instead.'

'But why does he have all those cages?' Maddie asked.

'They used to contain his mother's birds,' Poppy replied. 'She collected those as well as

143

china, apparently. When she died, Horace let them all go.'

'But if *Horace* didn't kidnap you, then who did?' Maddie asked.

'We still don't know that, which is why we need your help,' said Queen Flora. 'Maddie, I would like to introduce you to the other fairy queens.'.

Maddie gave the other fairies in the garden her full attention now. They were all very beautiful and each one had very large glittering wings.

'This is Queen Mae, queen of the oldest flower-fairy community – the one on the Isle of Skye in Scotland.'

Queen Mae was sitting on a little rug of yellow rose petals to protect her dress from grass stains. She wore a cream silk petticoat with an outer skirt of deep-pink petals and her bodice was made of woven lavender.

On top of her golden hair she wore a purple floral crown. 'Hello, Maddie,' she said, in the softest of Scottish voices.

'Hello,' Maddie said shyly.

'And this is Queen Amethyst . . .' Queen Flora continued, pointing to a very grand-looking fairy who was standing on the kitchen window sill looking down at everybody. She had long snow-white hair and she wore a long purple dress made out of crepe and tissue paper, which rustled when she moved. Her waistband was made from a purple velvet bookmark. She had gold spots on her dress and she wore a gold crown made out of all the different letters of the alphabet. Her shoes were purple too and they seemed to have little gold exclamation marks on them. She had sharp cheekbones and a pointed chin and her eyes were a very vivid violet colour.

'I am the queen of the book fairies,' she said.

'Did you find your entry-book at Mr Hatter's?' Maddie asked, remembering now that Mr Hatter had definitely taken *that*.

'Yes,' Queen Amethyst replied. 'He gave it back to us when we explained what it was.'

'He said that he only took it out of the library because the cover looked so interesting,' Poppy chipped in.

'It seemed a rather old, dull-looking cover to me,' declared another fairy who was sitting on the grass, basking in the moonlight. She had silky dark hair that fell to her waist, and cornflower-blue eyes. She was wearing a crown of real stars and her long floaty dress seemed to change colour from pale blue to dark blue to black as she sat there. As the dress became black it

146

began to sparkle with tiny shooting stars and Maddie couldn't help staring at it.

'This is Queen Celeste . . .' Queen Flora said.

Queen Celeste smiled the sweetest of smiles. 'I am queen of the dream fairies,' she said. 'I am very pleased to meet you, Maddie. Dream fairies don't get to meet human children very often, so this is a great honour.'

'It's an honour to meet you too,' Maddie said warmly.

'And last but not least, this is Queen Eldora, queen of the tooth fairies,' Queen Flora announced, introducing the last fairy queen who had long golden hair coiled up neatly on top of her head and a crown made from little tooth-shaped gold droplets. She wore a white trouser suit that was exactly the same colour as the whitest,

glossiest tooth enamel, and poking out of one of the pockets of her jacket was a gold toothbrush with bristles that sparkled.

'Normally different types of fairies don't mix with each other very much,' Queen Flora went on, 'but two tooth fairies and one dream fairy have also gone missing, as well as a book fairy and my flower fairies, so we have decided to join together in order to find them.'

'All of them disappeared while they were in this village,' Poppy put in.

'My missing book fairy, Emerald, is rather a nervous fairy and she has already had a number of unfortunate encounters with humans,' Queen Amethyst told Maddie. 'I fear this will make her even more nervy than she is already. We must find her quickly.'

'There is no time to waste,' agreed Queen Eldora, taking out her toothbrush

and flourishing it in the air as she spoke. 'My tooth fairies will be very frightened too. They were kidnapped while they were collecting teeth here two nights ago.'

'One of my dream fairies found a magic bed in this village last night and she hasn't been seen since,' Queen Celeste said.

Queen Flora turned to look at Maddie. 'Are you willing to help us?'

'Of course,' Maddie replied. 'But how?' If Mr Hatter hadn't got the missing fairies, Maddie couldn't think *where* to start looking for them.

'We need to find out if anyone in the village knows how to make bird-lime,' Queen Flora said. 'The person who does may well be the person we are looking for.'

'There can't be many humans who have even heard of it,' Queen Mae added.

'We need you to set a trap for this person, Maddie,' Queen Flora said, 'and we want you to use one of us as bait.'

'*Bait?*'

'That's right. You must go into the village first thing tomorrow and start telling everyone that you have a fairy queen in your possession. Hopefully the kidnapper will approach you if he thinks he's going to have the chance to add a fairy queen to his collection.'

'Yes, but then what?' Maddie asked anxiously. 'Do you want me to follow him and see where he's hiding the fairies?'

'No,' said Queen Flora firmly. 'This man might be dangerous for children as well as for fairies. You must certainly not go with him or try to follow him. Opal will be with you, and after he has revealed who he is, she will come and tell us.'

'Opal?' Maddie was surprised. 'What about Poppy?'

'Poppy won't be able to let us know as easily as Opal,' Queen Flora said. 'Besides, she is more delicate than the other fairies. I don't want to put her in a situation that she can't escape from easily if something goes wrong.'

Maddie glanced across at Poppy, who was looking very sulky. The word 'delicate' had reminded Maddie of how, when she was younger, her mother had been forever telling everyone that she was 'a delicate child'. It was true that she had been a very sickly baby, and had been much smaller than other children her age for several years until she had caught up, but she had never *felt* delicate and she had hated being called that.

'Yes, but Poppy's seen this man before,'

151

Maddie pointed out. 'She's the only one who can identify him for us. And we need to know for sure that the person who approaches me is the one who's stolen the fairies.'

The fairy queens looked at each other. 'She has a point,' Queen Mae said.

'Anyway, she'll be quite safe,' Maddie added quickly. 'She can sit in my pocket the whole time.'

'I have another idea,' Queen Eldora said suddenly. 'In Tooth-fairy Land we have a Wing Room where we grow false wings. Would Poppy like to come there and be fitted for one?'

Queen Flora looked at her in surprise. 'You never mentioned this before.'

'Well, we have never spent much time together before, have we?' Queen Eldora replied crisply.

Maddie looked at Poppy, thinking she would be thrilled by Queen Eldora's idea, but instead Poppy was looking alarmed. 'A *false* wing doesn't sound very nice,' she said doubtfully.

'Nonsense!' Queen Eldora said briskly. 'They work very nicely indeed if you spend some time learning how to use them.'

'They're probably not very *pretty* though, are they?' Poppy mumbled under her breath.

'It sounds like a marvellous idea to me, Poppy,' Queen Flora said enthusiastically. 'Though as I said just now, I had no idea that tooth fairies *had* such things!' She said it a little accusingly, as if she was still feeling a bit miffed that the tooth-fairy queen hadn't told her about her Wing Room before.

'Everything in Tooth-fairy Land is a

closely guarded secret,' Queen Eldora said firmly, 'but if you had told me before that you had a fairy with only one wing, then of course I would have offered to help her.'

'Well, at least she can be helped now,' Queen Mae put in quickly. 'Can you take her to Tooth-fairy Land tonight and fit her with a false wing so that she can wear it tomorrow?'

'Of course.'

But Poppy still looked worried. 'I don't know that I *want* a false wing,' she said. 'What will the other fairies say if I have a wing that's different to theirs? They might laugh at me – especially if I can't manage to fly very well with it.'

'That sounds like a very silly argument to me,' Queen Eldora replied impatiently. 'Surely having only one wing makes you different from the others in any case?'

'Yes, but everyone's *used* to me being like this. And ... and ... *I'm* used to it.' Poppy hung her head. 'Anyway, I don't want to go to Tooth-fairy Land tonight,' she said stubbornly. 'I want to stay here.'

Maddie thought she understood a bit of what Poppy was feeling. She remembered the first time she had used her inhaler in school – how worried she had been that people would stare at her.

'Why don't you give Poppy some time to think about it,' she said. 'And I'd really like it if she stayed here with *me* tonight. If she wants to, I mean.'

'Oh, yes,' Poppy responded, nodding enthusiastically.

'Very well, but only if you both agree to go straight back to bed and get plenty of sleep,' Queen Flora said. 'You both have an important day ahead.'

'You mean I *am* allowed to go with Maddie to catch the kidnapper?' Poppy blurted.

'Yes,' Queen Flora replied. 'Maddie is right – even though you can't fly, you are still the best fairy for the job. But Opal must go with you. Once you have identified the kidnapper, Opal can follow him.'

'We'll go straight to bed now, I promise, though I think I'm too excited to fall asleep again!' Maddie exclaimed.

'Falling asleep is easy,' Queen Amethyst told her briskly. 'All you have to do is read the right book.'

'The right book?' Maddie stifled a yawn.

Opal giggled. 'She means a *boring* one, of course!'

'Or if you prefer I can hum you to sleep with a dream-fairy lullaby,' Queen Celeste suggested. 'That is much *pleasanter* than reading a boring book.'

Queen Amethyst gave her a glare. 'Reading a book is a far more *natural* method for humans to get to sleep,' she said firmly.

'Uh . . . I think I'd rather just get to sleep on my own, thanks,' Maddie interrupted them quickly, beginning to see why different fairy types might not always get on. 'Come on, Poppy.' She crouched and lifted Poppy up on to her shoulder.

'Sleep well, Maddie,' Queen Flora told her. 'And take good care of Poppy, won't you?'

'We'll take care of each other,' Maddie said firmly, and she waved goodnight to Opal and the fairy queens as she headed back inside the house with her friend.

10

Poppy told Maddie that she wanted to sleep on the inside window sill, with the curtains open so she could look up at the stars.

'Aren't you afraid you'll roll over in the night and fall off?' Maddie asked as she folded up a fluffy hand towel to make a soft mattress for Poppy to lie on.

'No. Why? Are you afraid *you'll* roll over in the night and fall off *your* bed?'

'I suppose the window sill is as wide as a bed if you're fairy-sized,' Maddie agreed, seeing her point. But she put a pillow on the

floor under the window just in case. After all, a window ledge was a lot *higher* than a bed if you happened to fall off it, *especially* if you were fairy-sized.

As Maddie and Poppy lay in their respective beds, Maddie plucked up the courage to ask the question she had wanted to ask Poppy for ages. 'I've been wondering . . .' she began. 'How can a fairy be born with just one wing?'

Poppy sighed. 'Queen Flora says that it's very unusual and that it hardly ever happens, but something went wrong with me when I was in the process of being made. You see, fairies are made from bundles of joy that are brought to fairyland by special doves. The white doves deliver the bundles to the fairy nursery, where they grow into fairy babies.'

'That's amazing!'

'Anyway, the white dove who was

delivering *my* bundle of joy had an accident on the way,' Poppy continued.

'What sort of accident?'

'We don't know exactly, but Queen Flora says that when the dove arrived she was very upset and said that her bundle of joy had fallen to the ground during the flight and that she feared it was damaged.'

'That's terrible. But couldn't the fairies use their magic to make you better?'

'Queen Flora says that no magic is more powerful than the beginning magic. That's the magic that creates a fairy in the first place, and if anything goes wrong with that, Queen Flora says you can't do anything except take very good care of the baby fairy and just wait and see. And with me they soon saw that I was only ever going to grow one wing.'

'There was a girl in the next bed to me

in hospital,' Maddie said slowly. '*She* only had one hand. I thought she'd been in an accident or something, but she said she had been born that way.'

'Really?' Poppy looked very interested now. 'I didn't realize that sort of thing could happen to children as well as to fairies.'

'She was very brave about it,' Maddie told her. 'And she had an artificial hand that could do lots of things.'

'An *artificial* hand? Really? What did it look like?' Poppy was sitting up on the edge of the window ledge now. 'Did it look like a *real* hand?'

'Not exactly like a real one,' Maddie answered truthfully, 'but it looked fine. And she said it was much better than not having a hand at all.'

Poppy looked thoughtful. 'I couldn't believe it when Queen Eldora said she could give me a false wing. And when she offered to take me away with her to Tooth-fairy Land and completely change me overnight, I felt scared. Do you think that's silly?'

'Of course not,' Maddie said. 'It's very scary, having to go to a place you've never been before and get a new wing that will change how you look and everything . . . even if there is a chance that you'll be able to fly afterwards . . . which would be totally amazing of course . . .'

Poppy didn't speak for a few moments. Then she said, 'I guess it *would* be amazing to be able to fly, wouldn't it?'

'I think so,' Maddie agreed.

'I think maybe I *will* think a bit more about Queen Eldora's offer,' Poppy said, lying back down on her bed again. 'But not now . . . maybe tomorrow . . .'

'I suppose we ought to get some sleep

now,' Maddie said. But she had one more question before she closed her eyes. 'You know how you were telling me about the white doves bringing bundles of joy to the fairies so they can turn them into fairy babies? Well, where do the doves get the bundles *from* exactly?'

Maddie waited, but Poppy didn't reply.

'Poppy?' Maddie hissed into the dark. 'You can't have fallen asleep already!'

'It's a secret where the bundles of joy come from,' Poppy whispered back – and with that she shut her eyes and wouldn't say another word.

The following morning while they were having breakfast (Poppy was sitting next to Maddie's plate eating little pieces of toast and jam that Maddie kept breaking off for her) the doorbell rang.

Grandma went to answer it and to everyone's surprise it turned out to be Horace Hatter. 'Horace has brought back Maddie's library book,' Grandma said.

Sure enough, tucked under his arm was the book on butterflies which Maddie had taken out of the library. She had forgotten all about it.

'You left it on my hall table,' Horace grunted.

'Thank you,' Maddie said, standing up to take it from him. He must know that *she* knew that the fairies had paid him a visit, she thought, but his expression wasn't giving anything away. She noticed that Poppy had hidden behind the jam jar, despite knowing now that Horace wasn't the kidnapper.

Horace turned to Grandpa next. 'I'd like to apologize about your mother's ornament. I never should have taken it.'

'So why did you?' Grandpa asked bluntly.

'I was desperate to please my mother, I suppose,' Horace said.

There was an awkward silence while Grandpa continued to scowl at Horace.

'So *did* you please her?' Maddie asked

politely, when it seemed nobody else was going to speak.

Horace turned to her and slowly nodded. 'I think so. She wasn't an easy person to please, but she was happy that day, all right. I told her I'd found the ornament in a second-hand shop.'

'She must have known where it really came from,' Grandpa said sharply.

Horace nodded. 'I suppose she just chose to turn a blind eye. She was very passionate about her ornament collection, you see. More interested in that than anything else really – that and her bird collection, of course. I always reckoned her collections mattered to her even more than I did!' He gave a self-conscious little laugh.

'Your whole family was obsessed with collecting things,' Grandpa grunted.

'Completely bonkers, the lot of you, if you ask me.'

Maddie thought that sounded quite rude and she was starting to feel sorry for Mr Hatter. She was imagining what he must have felt like when he was a boy, having a mother and father who were more interested in their various collections than in him. 'I'm glad you let all the birds out of their cages after your mother died,' she told him.

Horace looked surprised, and her mother and grandparents stared at her.

'How do you know Mr Hatter did that, Maddie?' Mum asked.

She realized then that she only knew because the fairies had told her. 'Er . . .'

Luckily Horace started speaking again immediately. 'The only problem with me doing that was that those birds wouldn't be

167

used to fending for themselves. Goodness knows what became of them all. I didn't think about that when I let them go.'

'Why *did* you let them go?' Maddie asked curiously.

'Oh, I don't know. I just had this feeling that it was time they had their freedom, I suppose.'

'Well, they were very grateful,' Poppy piped up, stepping out from behind the pot of jam so that Horace could see her. 'We fairies looked out for them and helped them find new homes in the woods. Most of them settled in very well, although two of the canaries decided they wanted to emigrate to a warmer country so I'm not sure what became of them.'

Horace was staring at Poppy. He seemed about to answer her so Maddie cut in quickly, 'Mr Hatter, are you going into the

village just now? If you are, I'd like to come with you.'

'Maddie!' Mum said sharply. 'You know you can't go off into the village on your own.'

'I won't be on my own. I'll be with Mr Hatter.'

Maddie's mother and grandparents looked at each other, clearly not considering Mr Hatter to be a suitable companion, but not liking to say so in front of him.

'Why don't *you* go too?' Grandma said to Grandpa, giving him a nudge with her elbow. 'It's about time you and Horace made friends after all these years.'

Grandpa looked dubious, but Maddie had jumped out of her seat and was halfway to the door. Before anyone could say anything else, she had rushed upstairs to get her cardigan and her inhaler.

Poppy leaped on to her shoulder as soon as she came down to the kitchen again, and when Grandpa had finished his coffee they all set off. Milo, who had been let out into the garden while they were having breakfast, came too.

When they got outside they found Opal sitting on a wall waiting for them. 'We stayed over with Queen Flora last night,' she said. 'The fairy queens made me go to bed as soon as we got back and then they stayed up talking for the rest of the night, so now they're so tired they've had to go for morning naps. Here, Poppy.' She handed Poppy a tiny gold bag. 'Queen Flora sent you some fairy dust in case you need it.'

As they walked along the road Grandpa and Horace started talking about the old days, and Maddie hung back to talk to Poppy and Opal, who were now each sitting

in one of her pockets. Poppy was sitting astride Maddie's inhaler, complaining that it didn't make a very comfortable seat, and Opal suggested she use her bag of fairy dust as a cushion.

'What can you actually *do* with fairy dust?' Maddie asked them curiously.

'Oh, lots of things,' Poppy replied. 'But one of the things is that it stops bird-lime being sticky. We were always rescuing birds who were stuck to trees back in the old days when there were more trappers about.'

When they reached the village Grandpa stopped at the post office and tied Milo up outside, and Horace said he was going straight to the cafe to have his breakfast. Maddie guessed that it was time to do what she had come here to do, which was to tell as many people as possible about the fact that she had a fairy queen. But how was she going to do that in front of Grandpa without him thinking she had gone totally mad?

'Opal, I think we'd better split up,' she whispered. 'You go with Horace and tell him to spread the news about my fairy queen in the cafe. Poppy and I will stay here with Grandpa.'

So Opal flew off after Horace, and Maddie followed Grandpa into the post office, where she was surprised to find Jack, the driver of the garden-refuse truck.

'How's your mother?' Grandpa was asking him, speaking extra loudly.

'I'm just about to pop in and see her now,' Jack answered. 'She's not bad for ninety-four, though she's being driven mad by my brother Ted at the moment. He came to visit nearly a month ago and he's not showing any signs of leaving.' Jack suddenly noticed Maddie and said, 'Hello

again, young lady.' And he started to tell Grandpa how he had helped her rescue a fairy from the back of his truck.

Grandpa listened and nodded politely, even though Maddie knew he didn't believe a word of it, finally cutting in with, 'I saw Ted out in the woods last week, as a matter of fact. I said hello, but I don't think he recognised me. It's been years since we met.'

'Too busy looking for fairies most likely – though I bet they don't stick around for long if they see him first!'

Maddie's ears immediately pricked up. 'Why wouldn't they want to stick around if they saw him?'

Jack grimaced. 'Oh, our Ted's always been a bit strange ... a bit of a cold fish, if you like. All he's ever been interested in is making money – he's always got one

173

money-making scheme or other on the go. He seems to be getting worse as he gets older. At the moment my mother says he's been acting very secretive and spending a lot of time up in her attic. She's sure he's up to no good in there.'

'Jack, is your brother an *old* man?' Maddie asked, holding her breath.

Jack chuckled. 'Well, I don't reckon he'd think so, but he'll be seventy-five next year. He's ten years older than me.'

'And do you collect garden rubbish from your *mother's* garden as well as everybody else's?' Maddie asked excitedly.

'What's this, Maddie? Twenty questions?' Grandpa put in, but Jack answered her anyway.

'Of course I do – if there is any. I always stop at my mother's place for a cup of tea before I start work if I'm over this way.'

'Will you tell your brother ...' Maddie began nervously, '... will you tell him that I've been looking for fairies in the woods too, and that I've ... I've found a fairy queen and that she's ... she's ... staying with me at the moment.'

'Is she indeed?' Jack sounded impressed. 'Is this special treatment you're getting on account of rescuing that fairy the other day then?'

Grandpa was shaking his head in disbelief. 'What will you think of next, Maddie?'

The lady who ran the post office had heard her too, and now she started asking Maddie to describe this fairy queen, though it didn't sound to Maddie as if she really believed in fairies any more than Grandpa did.

They were still talking about it when

the next customer walked into the shop, and straight away Maddie saw that he was an elderly man who looked very similar to Jack.

'Ted,' Jack said immediately, 'I was just coming to see you and Mother.'

'Where's this girl who says she's got a fairy queen?' Ted demanded. 'I've just been in the cafe and they're all talking about it in there.'

As Poppy peered out over the side of Maddie's pocket she let out a frightened gasp – and Maddie knew that they had finally found their kidnapper.

11

Ted did look very much like Jack, Maddie thought, only a lot older and not nearly as friendly. No wonder Poppy had mistaken Jack for her captor when she'd first seen him from behind.

'*I'm* the one with the fairy queen,' she said loudly – just in case Ted was hard of hearing like his brother.

But Grandpa intervened then, putting a protective hand on Maddie's shoulder as Ted took a step towards her. 'There's no need to get all fired up now, Ted.

Maddie's got a very active imagination, that's all. It's just a game about fairies she's been playing. She didn't mean any harm.'

'A game?' Ted was looking directly at her.

'Grandpa just thinks that because *he* doesn't believe in fairies,' Maddie told Ted, trying not to sound as nervous as she felt.

'Maddie ...' Grandpa was starting to sound impatient.

Ted stood where he was, staring at Maddie for several moments before glancing again at Maddie's grandfather and leaving abruptly.

Horace had followed Ted from the cafe and was waiting just outside the door. As soon as Ted left the shop, Opal peered out from behind Horace's shoulder and Milo started yapping loudly.

'He's the one, Opal,' Poppy hissed at her. 'You'd better follow him! But don't let him see you!'

'Where do you think he's going?' Maddie asked Jack.

'Back home to my mother's, I imagine.'

Suddenly Maddie heard Horace asking, 'Do you think your mother would mind if I paid her a visit? There's a potion I need that I think she might have.'

Grandpa, who was sceptical of all remedies that didn't come via the chemist's shop, let out a little snigger. 'Got a wart you think the fairies might have a cure for, have you, Horace?' he teased, but Horace ignored him.

'Can Grandpa and I come too?' Maddie asked quickly.

'Of course! That would be grand!' Jack replied enthusiastically. 'Some fresh faces

179

are just what she needs to take her mind off Ted.'

'I'm not sure that Horace and I are all that fresh-faced ...' Grandpa began drily.

'Speak for yourself,' Horace retorted. And to Maddie's surprise, he actually gave a little chuckle.

'We can't stay long,' Grandpa said as Jack ushered them in through his mother's front door. Milo was left in the front garden with the gate closed and he immediately rushed up to the window and started barking. But they soon saw that he was barking at the cat on the window ledge, rather than at any fairies.

Jack's mother's house was dark with low ceilings and a strong smell of old cooking. As soon as the old lady had finished

welcoming them, she turned to Jack and said in an anxious voice, 'He came in just before you and went straight up to the attic. I keep asking him what he's got up there but he won't tell me. He knows I can't get up there myself. I need you to go and see what he's doing, Jack.'

Jack sighed. 'Do you want me to go now?'

She nodded.

'Can I go too?' Maddie asked, but Grandpa immediately glared at her and told her not to be so nosey.

As Maddie sat on the edge of her seat, certain that Jack was about to find the fairies up in the attic, Horace started to ask Jack's mother if she had ever come across a recipe for bird-lime.

'Well, it's funny you should ask that . . .' And she told them she had found one only

a couple of weeks before, written on the back of another old recipe she was using.

'Did Ted see it too?' Maddie asked.

'He was here when I found it, yes. The funny thing is that it disappeared that same day. I'd left it in the kitchen in the afternoon and when I went back in there that evening I couldn't find it again. I know it's a bad recipe and I meant to destroy it, but I couldn't until I'd copied out the one on the other side of the paper.'

Maddie looked at Horace. It was all fitting together now.

Jack came back into the room then, looking frustrated. 'He's locked the attic door from the inside. I can't get in.'

'Oh, I dare say he'll come down when he's hungry,' Jack's mother said. 'You may as well wait till then, I suppose. Go and put the kettle on, will you, Jack? I've a nice fruit cake in that tin on top of the fridge.'

Maddie could feel Poppy fidgeting inside her pocket. Then she saw Opal out of the corner of her eye, waving to her from the doorway, taking care not to be spotted by any of the adults in the room who believed in fairies.

'Can I use your bathroom, please?' Maddie asked Jack's mother politely.

'Of course, dear. It's upstairs, straight ahead across the landing.'

Maddie left the room, hoping that the tea and cake would keep the grown-ups distracted for a while. It wasn't that she didn't trust Jack and his mother to help her if she told them the truth, but she had a feeling it would be easier to *trick* Ted into letting her into the attic.

As Maddie passed through the hall she

glanced into the kitchen and saw some shelves with lots of different-coloured bottles lined up along them. Those must be all the potions and remedies that Jack's mother made, Maddie thought. And on one side of the room Maddie saw a large white sink – just like the one Poppy had described her kidnapper using.

Opal was hovering in the air beside the ladder that led up to the loft room, the door to which had been firmly closed. 'I'm sure the kidnapped fairies must be up there,' she whispered, 'but that horrible old man is in there too.'

'Ted!' Maddie called out – as quietly as she could so that the adults downstairs wouldn't hear. 'Do you want to buy my fairy queen?'

As Maddie had predicted, it didn't take long for Ted to unlock the door

and peer down at her. 'Oh, it's you, is it?' He had a greedy gleam in his eye as he asked, 'Have you got her with you?'

'No, but I can go and fetch her.'

'How much do you want for her?'

'I'll tell you after I've seen your collection of fairies.'

Ted looked wary. 'You're saying you just want to see them and then you'll sell her to me?'

'Yes.'

'Wait a minute.' Ted came down the ladder – taking care to shut the loft door behind him. 'Empty out your pockets,' he told her gruffly. 'I don't want you sneaking any fairy dust or other trickery into my loft.'

Maddie lifted Poppy out of her cardigan pocket along with her inhaler, and turned the other pocket inside out to show it was empty.

'*You* again!' Ted exclaimed, staring at Poppy. 'How did you get out of that sack?'

'I found her!' Maddie told him. Then she realized she couldn't sound too much like a friend of the fairies if she was going to make Ted believe she was willing to hand over her fairy queen to him. 'I'm trying to find someone to sell *her* to as well.'

Ted sneered at her. 'Well, I only want fairies with *two* wings, thanks! And she can stay down here when you come and look in my loft.'

'Oh no,' Maddie said. 'She's got to stay in my pocket. Otherwise she might run away.'

'You bet I'll run away!' Poppy added

obligingly. 'Just because you rescued me from that rubbish bag doesn't mean *you* own me now. I keep telling you that!' She scowled at Maddie.

'All right, you can bring her with you,' Ted grunted, 'but I'll check *her* pockets too.'

Maddie put back her inhaler and held Poppy up in the air so the fairy could empty out her pockets in front of Ted. Unfortunately Poppy had no time to conceal the bag of fairy dust and Ted grabbed it greedily.

As he touched it, the gold bag started to glow.

'What's it doing?' Ted demanded, starting to look worried.

'Fairy dust self-destructs if it gets into the hands of a bad human,' Poppy told him smugly.

And as she spoke the tiny bag exploded

into a mass of gold sparks which fizzed around Ted's face like a swarm of wasps.

'Get them away from me, you fairy minx!' Ted spluttered.

'Opal, go and tell Queen Flora where we are,' Maddie called out as she started to climb up the ladder with Poppy on her shoulder.

It was only then that Maddie remembered Queen Flora's instruction that she wasn't to chase after the kidnapper herself in case he was dangerous. But it was too late for that now. Ted was still busy trying to bat the prickly gold stars away from his eyes as she hauled herself up into the loft and closed the door behind her, quickly pulling the bolt across.

She found herself in a large attic room which had two windows in the roof, both of which were shut. The room was almost

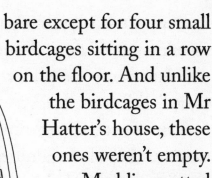

bare except for four small birdcages sitting in a row on the floor. And unlike the birdcages in Mr Hatter's house, these ones weren't empty. Maddie spotted Daisy and Primrose straight away. They had been placed together in one of the cages and now they were standing rattling the bars to get out. Next to their cage was another one that held a pretty blonde fairy in a pale blue dress. Two fairies in white dresses were calling to her from the third cage, and in the cage next to them was a very frightened-looking fairy in a bright green dress who Maddie guessed must be Emerald, the missing book fairy.

Poppy, who had remained on Maddie's shoulder until now shouted, 'Quick – put me down on the floor so I can go to them!'

Maddie set Poppy down in front of the cages and as she examined the door of the first one, she found to her surprise that it only had a very simple locking mechanism. There was something sticky on the lock though, and Maddie immediately saw why the fairies had been unable to lift the catches on their cages to let themselves out. All of the catches were smeared with bird-lime.

As she set to work undoing them, making her own hands sticky in the process, she heard Ted rapping on the other side of the loft door. He had obviously managed to escape from the explosion of fairy dust and had climbed up the ladder. 'I'm going

to fetch your grandfather if you don't come out,' he hissed at her. 'Then you'll be for it!'

Maddie realized that Ted was probably right. She *was* going to be in big trouble, especially as Grandpa wasn't going to believe her story that she had shut herself in the loft in order to rescue some fairies. But there was nothing she could do except hope for the best. Though if Ted kept making this much noise, the other grown-ups were bound to come upstairs to see what was happening sooner rather than later.

'Help them out of the cages, Poppy. But make sure you don't touch the bird-lime. I'll undo the windows and they can fly away.'

'They *can't* fly,' Poppy said. 'Look!'

Maddie turned to see that all the fairies' wings were covered in the same sticky green substance that had been on the cage doors.

'The old man put bird-lime on our wings so they'd stick together and we wouldn't be able to escape,' Daisy told them. 'None of us can fly now.'

Maddie immediately started to look around the loft for any sign of a sink or some water to wash off the bird-lime – but there was none.

'Haven't you brought any fairy dust with you?' Primrose asked Poppy.

'The old man found it, but don't worry. I've *never* been able to fly and that's never stopped *me* getting where I want to go. Maddie, open the window and lift me up.'

Maddie opened one of the skylight windows and lifted Poppy up on the palm of her hand. She watched as the fairy stood

balanced on the window frame, looking out into the afternoon sky. Almost immediately Poppy started whistling and waving her arms in the air as if she was trying to attract someone's attention.

'Are you hoping another fairy will see you?' Maddie asked. 'Opal will have gone to fetch the others, I expect, but I don't suppose they'll be able to get here for a while yet.'

'I know,' Poppy said. 'I'm not looking for a fairy.'

Suddenly a fat female starling landed on the roof beside the window, and Maddie realized at once what Poppy's plan was. The starling chirped at her and Poppy chirped back urgently in her best bird language. Then the starling flew straight off again towards a nearby tree.

'Don't tell me she won't help because

she's got to feed her babies,' Maddie gasped in dismay.

'No – don't worry. She's just gone to fetch some of her friends. Lift me back down to the floor again, will you, Maddie?'

The other fairies gathered round Poppy as she told them what was going to happen.

'The starlings will fly us straight to the fairy grove and we'll soon wash the bird-lime off your wings. But we must make sure we keep your sticky wings away from the starlings' feathers or *they* won't be able to fly either.'

'Poppy, you have to find Opal and Queen Flora and let them know that everyone is safe,' Maddie said. 'Otherwise they'll come here looking for you and Ted might catch *them* instead.'

'We'll let them know straight away,'

Poppy said. 'Don't worry about that. But what about you? Won't you be in trouble if you get found here?'

'Probably, but there's nothing I can do about that.'

Just then they heard footsteps on the landing below. 'Maddie? Are you up in that loft?' This time it was Grandpa, not Ted.

'Don't answer him,' Poppy whispered. 'I've got an idea!'

Suddenly there was a draught above them and a mad flapping of wings, as four starlings flew in through the open window to land on the loft floor.

'Quick!' Poppy cried out. 'Everybody climb on to a bird and hold on tight!'

Primrose and Daisy climbed on the back of the first bird and clutched its feathers very tightly as it took off. The two tooth fairies jumped on to the back of the next bird and

did the same. The dream fairy climbed up on to the third bird but Emerald, the book fairy, seemed too scared to join her.

'What if I fall off?' she said nervously.

'You won't so long as you hold on tight,' Poppy said firmly, and she shoved Emerald on to the back of the bird and told it to go.

Just as it was flying up and out of the window, they heard Grandpa's voice directly beneath them, sounding very stern now. 'Maddie, if you're up there—'

'Of course she's up there!' Ted's voice cut in angrily.

Maddie sighed. 'I guess it's time for me to let them in.'

'I don't see why you should,' Poppy replied. 'Take some puffs of your inhaler instead.'

'But I'm not breathless!' Maddie said,

though judging by the way her heart was beating she reckoned she soon would be.

'No, but if you want Ted to look really stupid, and you don't want to get into any trouble, you should do it!'

And although Maddie still didn't know what Poppy was talking about, something about the way she said it made her take out her inhaler and breathe in two puffs.

'I used some of that fairy dust to make a shrinking spell while I was inside your pocket,' Poppy told her. 'I thought you might need one today, so I put it inside your inhaler. Normally we just sprinkle shrinking spells over children's heads, but I reckoned it would work even faster if you actually breathed it in.'

Even as she spoke Maddie started to

feel dizzy. A weird tingling feeling was spreading across her body and her vision seemed to be going blurry.

'Shut your eyes. It's easier if you do,' Poppy instructed.

Ted and Grandpa were still shouting through the door at her as Maddie closed her eyes and felt her body tingling even more. It wasn't an unpleasant feeling – just a very odd one – and when she opened her eyes again she could hardly believe it. The loft was so huge it was unrecognizable and Poppy was the same size as Maddie. Even more alarming was the fact that the starling was the size of a small pony and its beak seemed very large and sharp.

'It's made you shrink down to the same size as a fairy, that's all,' Poppy said. 'Don't worry. It will wear off in a few minutes.'

Then Poppy was jumping on to the

starling's back and pulling Maddie up to
sit behind her. And before Maddie knew
what was happening, the bird took off with
a chirp and flew up out of the loft and into
the sky.

# 12

Everything went a bit crazy in Jack's mother's house after that. Rather unexpectedly, Ted got into such a frenzy that he called the local police and told them that some valuable property was in the process of being stolen from him. As the policeman arrived in his car, Maddie appeared from the back garden where she told everyone she had gone to get some fresh air. (She was now her normal size again, having been delivered safely back to earth by the starling.)

'You mean you weren't up in the loft at all?' Grandpa exclaimed.

'Who said I was up in the loft?' Maddie asked, doing her best to sound surprised.

Then Grandpa was turning on Ted and accusing him of lying, and Jack was explaining to the policeman that there had been a bit of a misunderstanding.

'At least there's no harm done,' Horace said, looking like he was quite enjoying all the excitement.

'Yes, there is,' Ted shouted, glaring at Maddie. 'She's stolen all my fairies!'

Everyone stared at him. 'What fairies?' Jack asked.

'The fairies I was going to sell on the Internet of course!' He sounded furious.

The policeman and Grandpa exchanged looks.

'Perhaps I should come in and have

a word, sir,' the policeman said to Ted. 'Claiming you've got *fairies* to sell over the Internet sounds rather fraudulent to me.' He gave Grandpa a wink as he guided Ted back into the house to question him some more.

'Come on, Maddie. I think it's time we went home,' Grandpa said, and Horace asked if he could walk back with them.

On the way Maddie slipped her hand into Grandpa's and said, 'I'm really sorry if I worried you, Grandpa.'

'It's my own fault, I suppose. I never even thought to check the garden. I just assumed you were in the loft like Ted said.'

'It wasn't your fault,' Maddie told him firmly.

'That policeman will have a fine story to tell his friends, in any case!' Horace said.

'He will that,' Grandpa agreed.

And after a moment or two, they all started to laugh.

That evening Maddie was looking out of the kitchen window as she helped Grandma with the dishes when she saw something glowing at the bottom of the garden. She guessed straight away that it was a fairy and she quickly finished drying the last few plates and went outside to look.

As she got closer she saw that the glow was rainbow-coloured and she found Queen Flora standing on the garden fence, waiting for her.

'Did all the fairies get home all right?' Maddie asked. 'And did you manage to wash the bird-lime off their wings?'

'Yes,' Queen Flora replied, smiling. 'Thanks to you they are all quite safe.'

'It's thanks to Poppy really,' Maddie said.

'It was her idea that we could all escape on the starlings' backs.'

'Poppy has made me very proud,' Queen Flora agreed. 'And tonight she has gone to Tooth-fairy Land with Queen Eldora to try out a false wing.'

'Oh, good,' Maddie said. Then she frowned. 'Queen Flora, I've been thinking about Ted. I mean, even though we stopped him this time – now that he knows the recipe for bird-lime, can't he just go out and catch more fairies whenever he wants?'

'He won't be able to. The other fairy queens and I are going to pay him a visit tonight while he is sleeping. We shall sprinkle a special spell on him – one that makes a human who believes in fairies *stop* believing in them. So you see, he won't have any reason to try to catch fairies again – here or anywhere else.' She sounded very

pleased by that thought. 'And now I have an invitation to give you. We would like to invite you to a party tomorrow night in the fairy grove. The party will be in your honour since it's your birthday.'

'Wow!' Then Maddie remembered what had happened the last time she had tried to go to a fairy party in the woods. 'But what about my mum?' she asked. 'If she wakes up and finds I've gone, she'll be really worried.'

'Why don't you bring her with you?' the fairy queen suggested.

'Really?' Maddie paused for a moment. 'But she'll never come. Not in the middle of the night! She just won't believe there *is* a party. Even if you sprinkle fairy dust to show us the way, she won't see it because she doesn't believe in fairies.'

Queen Flora thought for a moment.

'What if we light the way to the party with human lanterns instead?'

'Can you do that?'

'Of course. I shall send my fairies to borrow some! But no other humans must know about this party – just you and your mother.'

'I won't tell anyone,' Maddie promised. 'But I'm still not certain Mum will agree to come – even if she sees the lanterns.'

'Surely you can persuade her? She'll be in a good mood because it's your birthday, won't she?'

'Yes . . .' Maddie began slowly, 'but even though she's mostly happy on my birthday, I think . . . I think she always gets a bit sad at the same time because . . . because it makes her remember my twin sister and how it should have been her birthday too.'

'Poppy told me about your sister,' Queen

Flora said softly. She looked thoughtful for a few moments. 'Maddie, there is something I've been wondering whether or not to share with you ...' She paused. 'What exactly did Poppy tell you about how a fairy is made?'

'She told me they come from bundles of joy that the doves bring,' Maddie replied, 'but she wouldn't tell me where the bundles come from. She said that was a secret.'

'It *is* a secret,' Queen Flora said. 'But very occasionally a fairy queen may tell it to a child who is trusted. You see, the bundles of joy are made in a way that is difficult to understand ... a way that involves humans ...' She spoke very gently now, and the rhythm of her voice was so soft and mesmerizing that it made the little hairs on the back of Maddie's neck stand on end. 'What happens is this ... whenever a

human child dies anywhere in the world, all the happy energy that is contained within that child – all the energy that would have been used up during the child's lifetime – becomes what we call a bundle of joy. The bundles of joy are invisible to the human eye, but the doves collect them and bring them to us. Then we look after the bundles in our fairy nurseries until the beginning magic turns them into fairies.'

Maddie was staring at the fairy queen, hardly able to believe what she was hearing.

'There is one other thing you need to know, Maddie . . .' Queen Flora went on. 'A fairy can only live for as long as its special child is remembered by those that remain behind. Some fairies live for hundreds of years because memories of the human

child are passed down from generation to generation.'

Maddie swallowed. 'You mean . . .'

'I mean that somewhere in fairyland – and only the white doves know where – there is a fairy who is living because you and your family are remembering your sister.'

Maddie was totally stunned. After a moment or two she whispered, 'I'd really like to tell this to my mum.'

'You *may* tell her,' Queen Flora said softly, 'but only when you are both at the fairy party. So come at midnight and we will be waiting for you.'

Now all Maddie had to do was persuade her mother to go with her to the party. As the following day was Maddie's birthday she didn't really get the chance to ask her

mum, because she was kept so busy with all the things that had been arranged for her.

In the morning she had to open all her presents. Her gift from Aunt Rachel was a book called *The Fairy-Spotter's Guide*. It had beautiful pictures of lots of different sorts of fairies and tips about where to find them, but the person who had written it didn't seem to know about book fairies or dream fairies, Maddie noted.

At lunchtime Dad phoned to wish her happy birthday and they talked excitedly about all the things they would do when he came to spend the last fortnight of the holidays with them.

In the afternoon they went out for a lovely picnic tea, which was made extra-special by the fact that Grandma had made her a beautiful birthday cake with yellow icing and a sugar fairy sitting on the top.

(Milo tried to eat the fairy but they stopped him just in time.)

To everyone's surprise, Horace Hatter called by that evening, to wish her a happy birthday too and to give her a present. It was a box of chocolates, which Maddie decided she would take with her to the fairy party. Mr Hatter also mentioned that several of his garden lanterns seemed to have been stolen and that other people in

the village had reported missing lanterns too.

'Probably just kids mucking about,' Grandpa said.

'Or fairies,' Maddie added, grinning.

Horace also brought the news that he'd met Jack in the village that day, and that Jack's mother had finally ordered Ted to pack his bags and go back to his own home – which thankfully was quite far away. As Maddie walked Horace down the path to see him off he added in a low voice, 'She also found the recipe for bird-lime and destroyed it – though doubtless Ted has memorized it by now.'

'Don't worry about that,' Maddie whispered back. 'The fairies have made sure he won't ever want to use it again.'

At bed-time Maddie's mum came and sat with her and asked her if she'd had a nice

day. Maddie nodded and said it had been the best birthday ever. 'And I can't wait to see my new bicycle,' she added. Her parents had given her a bicycle after all, which Dad was going to bring with him when he came to stay. And he had also promised to spend lots of time teaching Maddie how to ride it safely.

'Don't worry, I'll be very careful when I'm riding it,' Maddie told her mum now.

'I know you will, darling,' Mum said, kissing the top of her head. 'I know it seems like I'm nagging sometimes but—'

'It's not just because of my asthma, is it, Mum?' Maddie interrupted her. 'It's because of Charlotte as well.'

'Oh, Maddie ... I don't want to make you afraid to do things ... It's just that that night when you were rushed into intensive care, it felt like ... like what happened

when you and Charlotte were born was happening all over again. It made me feel very frightened, and I guess it's taken me a while to stop feeling like that.'

'But it *wasn't* happening again, Mum,' Maddie said fiercely, and she gave her mother a big hug.

Mum hugged her back very tightly. 'I know. And I'm so proud of you, Maddie. I can hardly believe you're nine already!'

Then Maddie remembered that she still hadn't told Mum about the fairy party.

'Mum, I've got an idea,' she said, pulling back from her mother so she could see her face. 'You know how you told me that you and Aunt Rachel had lots of midnight feasts when you were little? Well, why don't you and I have one tonight, in the garden?'

Mum laughed. 'I think I'm a bit old for midnight feasts, Maddie.'

'Yes, but I'm not and I can't have one on my own, can I?'

Mum looked at her thoughtfully for a moment. 'You know, you're right. I guess I always had Rachel to do things like that with . . .'

'So does that mean we can have one?'

Mum nodded. 'But only if you get some sleep first. I'll come and wake you up at midnight, and if you still want to have a midnight feast then, we will. How's that?'

Maddie agreed excitedly, though she couldn't help feeling a bit worried that Mum might not wake her up after all when the time came. So she secretly made up her mind to stay awake herself until midnight, just in case.

## 13

As it happened, she needn't have worried. Just before midnight her mum came into her room and gently shook her awake, just as she'd promised. And it was just as well, because Maddie had fallen asleep an hour before, despite trying not to.

Maddie quickly dressed in the same party outfit she had worn the last time she'd tried to find the fairy party in the woods. She placed her sparkly shoes and the box of chocolates that Horace had given her into her bag, and all she had to

do then was put on her sandals and comb her hair.

'Goodness!' Mum said, when she saw what Maddie was wearing. 'You didn't tell me we were dressing up for this midnight feast.' Mum was still wearing her nightie and a thin cotton dressing-gown.

'I want us to have our midnight feast right at the *bottom* of the garden,' Maddie said. 'You'll need to get dressed and wear some proper shoes.'

'Oh, Maddie,' Mum said, stifling a yawn.

'*Please*, Mum!'

'Well, wait a minute then.'

'I'll meet you in the kitchen!' Maddie quickly picked up her inhaler (which thankfully no longer contained shrinking dust) and put it into her bag before she could forget it.

As she headed downstairs she paused outside her grandparents' bedroom. Milo was whining and scratching at the door as if he wanted to come to the party too, so very quietly Maddie opened the door to let him out. He burst out on to the landing wagging his tail excitedly, and Maddie had to tell him very sternly that if he wanted to come with them to see the fairies he would have to behave himself.

Maddie opened the back door while she waited for Mum to come downstairs and ran down to the bottom of the garden with Milo to see if she could see any lanterns. There was one hanging from a tree just on the other side of the garden gate. Maddie ran back to the house excitedly, leaving Milo sitting underneath the lantern.

'Come on, Mum,' she said, grabbing her hand as soon as she came into the kitchen.

'Come outside – there's something I want to show you.'

'Wait a minute,' Mum said, picking up Grandpa's torch from the table.

'It's OK, Mum – we won't need that.'

Maddie led her mother down to the bottom of the garden, where Milo was wagging his tail at them, eager to set off. When Mum saw the lantern hanging on the tree she assumed Maddie had put it there.

'No, Mum, it wasn't me. Let's see if there are any more.' Maddie led her mum through the gate and as soon as they were standing under the first lantern they saw the second one. Mum was curious now, Maddie could tell. The lanterns were leading them to the path they usually walked along with Milo, and when they reached it they both stared in amazement.

Lanterns had been placed along both sides of the path, making a walkway for them.

'I can't believe this,' Mum murmured, sounding totally awed. 'Who's done all this?'

'Come on, let's follow it,' Maddie whispered, and she led the way along the lantern-lit walkway which soon guided them off the main path and in among the trees. Milo was starting to yap with excitement now and Maddie had to tell him to be quiet.

'The fairies must have borrowed *hundreds* of lanterns,' Maddie exclaimed, when they had been walking for several minutes and the lantern pathway was still flickering ahead of them for as far as they could see.

'The *fairies*?' Mum sounded incredulous.

The lantern path led them all the way
to the stream and when they got there the
water was sparkling brightly. Mum looked

like she was in a daze as they followed the lanterns along the edge of the water towards the fairy grove.

There Mum stopped abruptly and drew in her breath. In the little clearing, lanterns of all different colours had been hung from every tree. The ground was also sparkling with fairy dust (though Maddie guessed Mum couldn't see that), and a large rug made from petals had been spread out in the middle of the grass.

Milo began to bark and suddenly a tree stump on the edge of the clearing began to glow and a second or two later the most magnificent rainbow shot out of it, stretching up through the trees into the night sky. Out of the base of the rainbow flew dozens of flower fairies, each one wearing a different brightly coloured petal dress.

'*That's* the entrance to fairyland!' Maddie exclaimed.

Mum couldn't see the fairies or the rainbow, but there were lots of different woodland animals gathering in the clearing now – birds of all kinds, rabbits, hedgehogs, squirrels, field mice, moles and even a badger – and Mum could clearly see those.

'I must be dreaming,' Mum murmured as she stared in total shock at the scene around her.

Milo clearly thought he was dreaming too, because instead of chasing the animals like he would normally do, he stood frozen to the spot, wagging his tail at them.

'You'd better sit your mother down,' a familiar fairy voice suddenly said from behind them. 'She'll fall asleep soon.'

Maddie turned and saw Poppy, only her fairy friend was actually *flying*! She

was wearing a new poppy-petal dress with extra sparkles on it and her one real wing was sparkling now as it flapped behind her. Her new false wing was flapping too. 'What do you think?' she asked Maddie, giving a little twirl in mid-air. The false wing was larger and a bit more solid-looking than the other one, but it looked quite pretty just the same and it had red sparkles on it to match Poppy's dress. 'Queen Eldora has given it to me as a present for helping to rescue her tooth fairies.'

'It looks great – but is it difficult to fly

with?' Maddie asked, because she knew
that had been one of Poppy's main fears.

'Not really, though my own wing isn't
used to flapping so it's quite weak still,
whereas the new one flaps very strongly. I
have to be a bit careful or I end up going
round in circles. But I think it's going to
get easier the more I practise.'

Mum was sitting down on the petal rug
now, looking sleepy.

'Pretty soon she'll fall asleep and then
she'll wake up and tell herself it was all a
dream,' Poppy said. 'That's what she did
when she was a little girl too.'

'I have to speak to her first,' Maddie
said, sitting down on the rug beside her
mother.

'I'm so tired,' Mum mumbled, starting to
close her eyes.

'I know, Mum, but there's something

225

important I have to tell you before you go to sleep.'

Very gently she started to tell her mother what Queen Flora had told her about how fairies were made.

Mum listened, and as she did, her eyes began to glisten with tears. 'Fairies are really our most precious memories then . . . the memories of our lost children . . . is that what you're saying?'

'Well . . .' Maddie was taken aback. She wasn't sure that that *was* what Queen Flora had meant, though she guessed it was sort of right since a fairy could only live for as long as someone still remembered that fairy's special child.

'That's a very beautiful, comforting idea, darling,' Mum added softly.

'It's not just an *idea*, Mum,' Maddie said. 'It's what really happens. The fairies are all around you, if only you'd believe in them.'

But Mum's head was resting on the rug now and her eyes were closed. 'I'm glad *you* believe in them, Maddie,' she murmured, just before she fell asleep.

Maddie looked up a few moments later to see Queen Flora flying towards her. 'Don't worry about your mother, Maddie. She will wake up in her own bed tomorrow morning – we will see to that.'

'Then she really *will* think this has just been a dream,' Maddie pointed out.

Queen Flora smiled. 'With some grown-ups that can be the easiest thing,' she replied. 'Don't worry – she *did* take in what you told her, but in her own way, that's all. Now – let us get on with our party!'

'Where's Milo?' Maddie asked, suddenly noticing he wasn't with them.

'He's found the food,' Queen Flora said, smiling.

As Maddie looked round she saw that several fairies were bringing plates of delicious-looking sparkly food to a cluster of round tables at one side of the clearing and that one of them was feeding titbits to a very happy Milo. Maddie went over to join them and saw that the tables were actually large toadstools.

There weren't just flower fairies at the party, Maddie realized now. There were also tooth fairies, book fairies and dream fairies, and to her surprise there were boy fairies as well as girl ones.

Queen Celeste's dream fairies had set up an orchestra under one of the trees and they were playing some music that didn't sound

at all lullaby-ish. Queen Flora flew off to speak to them and they stopped playing dance music and started to play 'Happy Birthday to You!' instead.

As all the fairies gathered round, Queen Flora and the other fairy queens appeared in the centre of the crowd, carrying a birthday cake that was just the right size for Maddie. The cake had rainbow-coloured icing that sparkled, nine pink candles and in the centre there was a fairy who looked very like the sugar fairy on Grandma's cake except that she was sitting on a pink sugar

throne, waving to everyone and singing 'Happy Birthday to You!' along with them.

'It's beautiful!' Maddie gasped. 'Thank you.'

Poppy, Daisy and Primrose appeared then, each carrying a tiny bottle of sparkly liquid and a thimble-sized acorn cup.

'Try some of this, Maddie,' Poppy said. 'It's called bubbly dew. We make it ourselves and it's delicious!' She poured out a drink for Maddie and it *was* delicious – sort of sweet and fizzy and not at all like any other drink Maddie had ever tasted.

'Oh, I almost forgot. I've brought a box of chocolates with me,' Maddie said, taking them out of her bag. At the same time she took out her sparkly shoes. 'You couldn't shrink me again like you did yesterday, could you, Poppy?' she asked hopefully. 'Then I'd be the right size for your party.'

230

'Oh no!' Poppy exclaimed. 'We're not allowed to shrink children unless there's a very good reason.' She waited for Maddie to put on her party shoes, then added, 'And we absolutely *never* shrink chocolates.'

As the chocolate box was opened, Maddie found herself surrounded by fairies of all kinds, all eager to have a bite out of one of the sweets. There was a little bit of pushing and shoving, but no real arguing and all the fairies seemed to be willing to share with each other.

'Queen Flora says this is the first time there's ever been a fairy party where so many different kinds of fairies have all mixed together,' Poppy said. 'We never usually get on as well as this. I guess being kidnapped has brought us all much closer.' She waved to Opal and Emerald who were dancing nearby with some tooth

fairies and dream fairies. 'Shall *we* dance too?'

'I think I'm too big to dance with you, aren't I?' Maddie said.

'Not if you dance at the edge and watch where you put your feet,' Poppy replied.

So they went to dance with the others and Maddie took great care not to tread on any fairies. They were soon joined by a group of rabbits who were also keen to dance, thumping their hind-feet very vigorously against the ground in time to the music. Milo normally liked to chase rabbits, but tonight he seemed to just want to dance with them. Soon he was wagging his tail and thumping his back paws along with his new friends.

'This is the strangest party I've ever been to!' Maddie said, laughing.

'It's the strangest one *I've* ever been

to too!' Poppy told her. 'Fairies don't usually invite humans to their parties, you see.'

All the other fairies agreed that having a human at their party was very strange indeed – but that it was so much fun that they really must do it more often.

'You could invite Horace Hatter next,' Maddie suggested. 'I'm sure he doesn't get invited to very many parties.'

So Poppy said that she would ask Horace to the next fairy party they held in the woods. 'I wonder if *he'll* bring any chocolate with him,' she added, licking her lips.

And Maddie laughed and promised to remind him.

# A selected list of titles available from
# Macmillan Children's Books

The prices shown below are correct at the time of going to press. However, Macmillan Publishers reserves the right to show new retail prices on covers, which may differ from those previously advertised.

---

**Gwyneth Rees**

| | | |
|---|---|---|
| Mermaid Magic (3 books in 1) | 978-0-330-42632-9 | £4.99 |
| Fairy Dust | 978-0-330-41554-5 | £4.99 |
| Fairy Treasure | 978-0-330-43730-1 | £4.99 |
| Fairy Dreams | 978-0-330-43476-8 | £4.99 |
| Fairy Gold | 978-0-330-43938-1 | £4.99 |
| Cosmo and the Magic Sneeze | 978-0-330-43729-5 | £4.99 |
| Cosmo and the Great Witch Escape | 978-0-330-43733-2 | £4.99 |

*For older readers*

| | | |
|---|---|---|
| The Mum Hunt | 978-0-330-41012-0 | £4.99 |
| The Mum Detective | 978-0-330-43453-9 | £4.99 |
| My Mum's from Planet Pluto | 978-0-330-43728-8 | £4.99 |
| The Making of May | 978-0-330-43732-5 | £4.99 |

---

All Pan Macmillan titles can be ordered from our website, www.panmacmillan.com, or from your local bookshop and are also available by post from:

**Bookpost, PO Box 29, Douglas, Isle of Man IM99 1BQ**
Credit cards accepted. For details:
Telephone: 01624 677237
Fax: 01624 670923
Email: bookshop@enterprise.net
www.bookpost.co.uk

**Free postage and packing in the United Kingdom**